THE
PLANET

J SWIFT

Copyright © 2017 J Swift

Cover designed by MiblArt

ISBN:

For the Weirdo Squad.
I couldn't have made it through this without you.

CHAPTER ONE

ALISSA STARED AT THE BODY IN THE BOX. HIS EYES WERE closed, and he didn't even look like he was breathing. She had been sitting by Garret's bedside for hours now, ever since Megan had set up one of the medical-grade stasis chambers for him.

Seven volunteers had scavenged all the equipment they could from the infirmary on board the Ark, including their emergency generators. They would keep the chamber running for at least a week. After that, Garret was on his own.

He looked so small; the mere sight of him like this broke Alissa's heart. She had always considered him to be strong and dependable. But now here he was. Silent, unmoving, dying.

As she sat, Alissa heard a cough behind her. Someone was clearing their throat, making their presence known to her whether she liked it or not. She turned on her chair and eyed up the visitor. It was Shem. He stood there, not really looking at Garret and avoiding Alissa's stare while he picked at the rip in his sleeve. 'How is he doing?'

'Megan says he's healing in there but not fast enough. If the pod runs out of power before he's healed, he'll die.'

Shem nodded and watched Alissa as she turned back to face the small window in the pod. He was a fool not to realise how much she cared about Garret. He had been so wrapped up in his own issues, and the brig had taken so much from their friendship. Alissa was becoming someone new, and he felt like he had missed half the journey.

'Al, I've been sent by the survivors.' She didn't turn around. 'Look, we had a meeting about an hour ago. Megan told you about it, remember?'

Shem heard a deep breath being sucked in and released before Alissa tried to speak. 'I'm sad, Shem. Not an idiot.'

'Right, well, there are seven hundred and thirty-two survivors that we can account for. A lot of them are civilians, but there are some members of crew as well.' He paused, to see if Alissa had any questions, but she just stared at the chamber, so Shem carried on. 'There are only three surviving Chiefs. Brown and Colfer both hold the position, but it was a shared position among Nav officers. Their teams were small, and they don't feel comfortable with the responsibility of leading the survivors. The third is you. You ran the ship-wide security. People voted, and they're looking to you for leadership.'

Alissa closed her eyes, and a tear rolled down her cheek.

Shem could see her long brown hair cascade down her back, but all he could hear were her shallow breaths.

The security chief had been afraid of this. With her title, people felt safe around her. Alissa, the woman who allowed Vincent Stadler to roam free, allowed Captain Andover to die, lured the ship into an alien ambush, and lost almost all the people on board to violent deaths. How could that be the person they wanted to lead them?

'Alissa? They want to see you.' Shem's voice was soft, gentle. He was moving closer to her, reaching out his arm until his hand rested gently on her shoulder. Just as he made contact with her, Alissa rose to her feet and slowly turned to face him, closing the gap between them and taking both his hands in hers.

'I can't do this, Shem. I can't stand in front of those people and pretend I'm a leader. They're stranded here because of me.'

Shem was shaking his head while Alissa talked.

'Please, Shem. I can't watch while everyone…'

'While everyone slowly starves to death in front of you?' Shem finished her thought, and Alissa looked up at him with confusion.

'Come on, Al. Doesn't take a genius to figure out. There aren't enough supplies for everyone, and we landed on a barren desert of a planet. We're not gonna survive this.'

Alissa could see his eyes starting to well up with tears.

'Al, do you know what seven hundred people would look like if they lost hope?'

She shook her head. 'I don't plan on finding out, Shem. I'm gonna run. Grab some supplies and get out of here. I'd rather die alone.'

Shem bit his lip as he shook his head. 'Then you're a coward.'

'What?' Alissa stood there, open-mouthed at his stinging words.

'If you walk away from this, then you're a coward, Al. Those people need you.'

'What about what I need?' Alissa's eyes were beginning to water.

'This isn't about you!' Shem's voice was getting louder. 'This is about all of us, and we need a strong voice to keep people from losing their minds over this!' He took a step towards her, reached his arm out to her shoulder but Alissa shrugged it away.

'I can't stand in front of them and lie about all of this, Shem. It's all my fault.'

Shem stepped even closer and wrapped his arms around Alissa. This time she didn't pull away. She let his embrace comfort her. 'Just…be you, Al'

With his arm around her shoulder, Shem guided her out of the area but took one last look over her shoulder at the man in the stasis pod. They walked out of the small section they had cordoned off and crossed the wreckage to where the survivors had gathered.

***

There was silence. No one spoke a word as Alissa climbed up part of the broken ship and made her way onto the makeshift stage. Standing there already was Megan and Japheth. Shem followed behind Alissa. Everyone just watched as she walked. A palpable tension was in the air, and it made the security chief feel very exposed.

She reached the centre of the open stage and looked out at the crowd. Although it was only a small number in comparison to the total manifest of The Ark, it was still more people than Alissa had ever spoken to at once. She felt like her legs would give way any second as she stood there, staring at the people who in turn stared back at the woman they expected to save them.

With a cough, Alissa cleared the tickle from the back of her throat. 'I don't know what to say to you.' Her voice was as loud as she could make it, but in the open air, it didn't carry very far. The crowd began to whisper her words to each other as she spoke.

'I'm sorry this happened. I expect you must all know by now, but The Ark was attacked by an alien race that wants to destroy humanity. They are responsible for the destruction of every Ark since the initiative's inception. They are responsible for the captain's death.' Alissa paused to let the words be passed around the crowd. 'But so am I.'

Japheth whirled on the spot to look at Alissa as she spoke.

'I was taken captive into a facility that set me on a mission to assassinate Clarke Andover.'

Megan was staring at Alissa with her mouth hanging open. There was an untold rule between them, so Alissa had never mentioned the work Silver Glove tried to make her do and Megan never asked.

'It's only thanks to my friend Ham that The Ark made it safely off Earth.' Alissa scanned the crowd to see if she could spot her friend, but it was difficult to pick out one face in the mass. 'I convinced Garret to take the ship into unknown danger so I could save one man from being tortured by aliens, and that decision has led us here. To this moment.'

Another pause while the words sunk in around her.

'I'm not your leader. I'm the reason you're trapped here. I'm the reason people are dead, and I'm the reason you'll all starve to death on this rock.'

Alissa turned on her heel and crossed the stage to leave as people began to shout. Some shed tears while others wanted blood.

Shem followed closely behind her while Ham, who had watched from the side-lines, pushed his way through people to get to his friends.

Megan stood helplessly as Japheth crossed the stage to follow Alissa, but as the crowd moved in to stop her, his path was blocked.

'Alissa!' a voice called loudly behind her, enough so that she turned to look. It was Danny Colfer, one of the nav chiefs, followed by as many of the survivors as could squeeze through the tall chunks of metallic skeleton. 'Is all that true?' Colfer's eyebrows were almost touching in the middle. 'Is all this really your fault?'

Shem jumped in before Alissa could. 'How can you even ask that?'

Alissa took Shem by the hand. 'It's all right, Shem.' She turned to Colfer. 'Yes. It's true. I've been brainwashed and manipulated for months. I'm a dangerous person to have around.'

The crowd began to surround the three, closing in to hear as much as possible.

Colfer nodded. 'Alissa…I don't know what to say.'

She smiled bitterly. 'Well, make it poignant because I think you're in charge now.'

'Right…' His face was pale. 'Alissa, you risked the safety of everyone on the Ark, and we lost thousands of friends, family, and colleagues in the process.'

Alissa looked down at her feet while he spoke.

'We can't guarantee that you're not still under the control of the aliens…so I need you to leave.'

His voice was so gentle considering his words were so harsh.

Some people in the surrounding group cheered, and others stood there silently, just watching.

Alissa looked up into Danny's eyes. 'I understand, Colfer.'

'Good. Then you understand that you weren't on this mission alone. Shem Mitchell and—' He paused, for a second. 'I'm sorry I only know him as Ham. They were both part of your plan.'

Alissa looked up. 'Don't do this, Colfer, please. Don't.'

'All three of you are to leave this colony today and to take only what belongs to you. You're banished from this camp.'

Alissa's eyes lost focus as Shem put his arm around her shoulder. 'Please, man. Don't do this to Ham. He only came with us because he loves us, but you're condemning him to death if you banish him.'

'My mind is made up, Shem. You've made your choices and they led us here. So I'm doing this to protect those of us that remain.' Colfer turned and began working his way back through the people who were still looking on.

Alissa finally let the tears fall, and Shem held her for a few seconds, until he heard a quiet voice from behind him. 'Banished? I don't understand, Shem. Why are we banished?'

Shem turned and looked at his friend. 'Because they don't understand what we were trying to do.' He motioned towards Ham, and the big guy walked into Shem's outstretched arm. The three of them stood there for a while, in silence. Just holding each other.

CHAPTER TWO

'RIGHT, YOU EACH HAVE A PACK WITH A TORCH, BASIC   rations, rope, and a flare. Shem, you've got the emergency medical kit. It's not much, but it might save your life.' Megan smiled gently as she spoke, desperately trying to hide her watery eyes.

Shem looked at the small metal container in his hands. 'How did you manage to sneak this away?'

Megan smiled. 'They let the only living doctor do the stock check. And I made sure there were emergency supplies no one knew about.'

Alissa looked at her pregnant friend. Her bump was so pronounced now. She was due in two months, and Alissa would miss it. She would miss all of it. With a quiet sob, Alissa pulled Megan in for a hug, who let out a squeal of surprise before wrapping her own arms around Alissa.

'You'll be okay, Al. I won't stop fighting your case here. We will find a way to survive, and we will bring the three of you back. I promise.'

The women stepped away from each other, and Ham, Shem, and Alissa turned to begin their journey.

Within moments, Alissa heard her name being called, and the three of them turned to face the voice. 'Japheth.' His name fell from her lips.

He ran straight to Alissa and pulled her into an embrace. 'I'm coming with you. Everything you did, you did for me.' His handsome eyes were filled with worry as he looked down at Alissa. She shook her head.

'I need you here, with Megan. Keep her safe for me. You're the only one left here that I trust.'

'I don't want to lose you.' His voice cracked slightly.

'I know and I'm sorry.'

Japheth wrapped his arms around Alissa and pulled her in close. 'We can still talk, at night, in your dreams.'

Alissa pulled back slightly. 'No, we can't. You need to let me go and focus on what's going on here.'

'Al, please…'

'No, Japheth. I don't want you to watch me die.'

Gently, Japheth lifted her chin and gently kissed her. Alissa allowed herself to sink into the familiar comfort he provided. She wrapped her arms around him and pretended all this was a dream.

Shem turned away and started their long walk alone.

***

Night fell quickly in the desert. The three had walked for seven hours and seen no plants or animals. Not even insects. The land was completely barren.

'Okay, we rest here.' Shem dropped his pack and started unrolling the tent he had found in the supplies cupboard in the wreckage. 'I'll make shelter.'

He moved away from Ham and Alissa and silently started putting the rods through the fabric.

Alissa and Ham sat on the warm sand, and each took a sip of water from a bottle Alissa had. She placed it next to her, ready for Shem.

'He hates me.'

Ham looked at Alissa. 'Who does?'

'Shem! He's barely spoken to me since we left. He blames me for all of this.'

'No, he doesn't.'

'Then why is he being like this?'

'You kissed Japheth.'

Alissa froze. 'He kissed me.'

Ham smiled. 'Doesn't matter. You know how Shem feels about you, right?'

'Yeah, I do.'

'You hurt his feelings.'

Alissa leaned back on her arms. They would never see Japheth again, so what was one last kiss? It was their goodbye. Shem couldn't be jealous of a man that she would never speak to again. It was unreasonable.

She watched him as he put the finishing touches on the tent and came back to the group. He picked up the water and took a sip.

'So, how long do you think we can last out here?'

'Well.' Alissa thought back to the training Garret had given her. 'We have enough food rations to last us about two weeks. But if we don't find another source of water, we will run out in about thirty-eight hours.' Alissa looked at Shem. 'We won't last much longer after that.'

***

15

'Okay, civilians, you're now honorary crew. We are in this together.' After his conversation with Alissa, the crowd had fallen in behind Colfer. He would keep them safe as best as he could, but his plan was to wake up Garret as soon as possible and let him take over. Being responsible for all these lives was something that made him feel physically sick.

In the centre of the makeshift stage, Colfer looked out at the faces of the survivors, each one gazing hopefully up at him. 'Right, the first thing we need is power. Then we can try and get medical equipment working, maybe even some of the ships systems could be cannibalised and used to help build ourselves somewhere to live.'

'You're wrong.' A shout to undermine Colfer, in front of everyone.

He gritted his teeth. 'Who said that?' He scanned the crowd again. 'Well?'

'I said, you're wrong, Colfer.' Japheth had made his way to the front and was looking up at the navigation chief. 'Look, I've never worked on a ship, and I don't know much about survival but—'

Colfer cut him off. 'That's right. You have no experience so who the Hell are you to tell me I'm wrong?'

'It just seems to me that if we don't find food and water, then having a nightlight won't help much. We will be dead in days.'

The last sentence he whispered, hoping only Colfer would hear. The nav chief, who was now crouched at the edge of the platform to listen to Japheth, started to go pale.

He straightened up and looked back at confused faces. 'Food and water, those need to be the priority. But I want a team to keep looking for power. I have some ideas.'

***

It took a few hours, but eventually the survivors had split into three groups. One group was responsible for finding food, one water, and the third group was to find power. Colfer, Japheth, and Megan sat in the remains of one of the crew quarters, a representative from each group.

'So, how do we do this?' Colfer left the floor open for the other two to jump in.

'Well,' Megan began, 'The Ark used to have vast hydroponics bays, for oxygen and food. With a bit of luck, we may be able to find where that section crashed and salvage equipment for long term food growth. For the short term, my team has split into groups of ten and are searching all surrounding wreckage for food and rations. Specifically, they're looking for the food stores we had on board.'

Colfer nodded. 'Okay, good. And how much food do we currently have?'

'Well, we did a roundup this morning. We have enough to feed all the survivors for ten days.'

'And water?' He turned to Japheth who sat confidently. 'We are using part of the emergency power packs to scan the planet around us. We are hoping to find a natural source of water. However, it seems unlikely. The Ark did have a water recycling system, but it's damaged beyond repair. What we can do is take the system itself and build a smaller version of it. It's not the most pleasant, but it'll keep us alive. Until that's up and running, we only have one surviving water tank that will last eleven days if it's strictly rationed.'

Colfer nodded again. He was beginning to feel like all he ever did was just nod at the people around him. 'We are piggybacking your scans of the planet to look for power sources. Natural energy we can use. If we don't get some form of power within the next few days, Garret will likely die, and to be honest. I'd really like to avoid that if I can.'

This was a tough job, and he just wanted to hand it off to anyone that would take it. But it was his, for now.

***

Alissa shivered against the cold night air and wrapped herself up tighter in her blanket. There was no real protection from the cold, and nothing to fuel a fire. All they had was woollen sheets given to them as a part of their survival kits.

It wasn't cold enough to freeze, but it felt like it, being that the sun was so bright, and they had marched for hours through the sweltering heat. Comparatively, the night air was ice cold.

Ham's gentle breathing soothed Alissa, and she closed her eyes. Eventually they would succumb to the elements out here, but not tonight.

As the dawn began to break, Alissa was awoken by Shem gently shaking her shoulder. 'Come on, Al. We gotta get moving.'

She groaned and rolled over. 'Why bother? Either we die here, or we die fifty miles away from here. Either way, we are going to die.'

The stifled sob that came next broke her heart. As Alissa opened her eyes, Ham was shuffling out of the tent.

'Well done, Al. You wanna piss anyone else off?'

She stared daggers at him as Shem followed Ham out of the opening.

This was her punishment, for all the things she had done. Now she would die knowing her only friends hated her. Alissa rubbed her eyes until little silver stars danced in the darkness of her eyelids. Then she crawled out into the new day.

Ham and Shem sat on the sand eating a couple of pieces of their dried ration packs in silence. Alissa joined them and opened her own. 'I'm really sorry, Ham,' she mumbled as she chewed.

The three of them sat in silence for the rest of their breakfast, looking out at the white sun. It was another cloudless day, and they were all starting to smell quite ripe. Alissa prayed they would find water today.

They packed down the tent and began to walk again. There was no general chatter. The unspoken rule now was to conserve energy where they could. At a little before midday, they stopped to eat a few more rations and shelter from the hot sun. Shem built the tent while Ham and Alissa watched. Once it was ready, they clamoured inside and again ate a few pieces of their rations, this time with some water. Ham took a swig first, followed by Alissa. Once the cool liquid hit her tongue, it took every effort not to swallow every drop. Shem took the bottle next, and as he swallowed his mouthful, he frowned. 'The water's getting real low.'

CHAPTER THREE

WITHOUT KNOWING IT, COLFER HAD TAKEN ALISSA'S   place beside Garret's bedside, praying for a miracle. Something to keep Garret alive. He sat there for hours just watching, hoping that he would see an eyelid flicker or a finger twitch. Just something to give him solid hope.

***

'Megan, could you stop pacing, for just a minute and calm down?' Japheth watched her cross back and forth across the sand. 'You're a doctor, surely you know that you'll dehydrate if you keep this up.'

She stopped. Staring out into the distance, the direction Ham, Shem, and Alissa had gone. 'With the rations they left with, they won't have long left.' She turned to look at Japheth, who was sitting on a chunk of the Ark. 'They're really going to die out there.'

20

'We will find a way to bring them back. I promise.'

'Bring them back to what? We're all going to die here, Japheth. I don't want to lose my baby.' Tears fell freely from her eyes as Japheth looked on. He slid off the metal and put an arm around her shoulder.

'Listen, I made a promise that I would keep you safe. That's what I'm gonna do. No matter what, you and the baby are gonna survive this.'

***

'Colfer?'

The chief turned slowly in the chair to see who had bothered him. It was one of the younger technicians. No more than twenty. Probably took the test early and was granted access. *Smart-ass.*

'What is it?'

'Sir, the scans running from the shuttle. They've found something.'

Colfer leapt up and almost lifted the tech off his feet as he gripped his overalls. 'What is it? What did they find?'

'It's a power source. Coming from pretty deep underground.'

***

Colfer sat in the remains of the crew quarters. This had quickly become their meeting room. An ideal location, quiet and off the beaten track so none of the survivors came by. They could speak freely.

'How deep underground?' Megan had sat herself on the burned remains of the bed and shuffled slightly as she asked.

'They think it's at least two miles.'

21

'What!' Japheth stood leaning against the old doorframe with his arms folded. 'How in the Hell are we supposed to dig two miles down in dry sand with no technology?'

Colfer wasn't making eye contact with either of them; he stared at a hangnail on his thumb. 'If we want to live, we will have to find a way.'

'So, what's your plan?' Megan asked softly.

'I don't know.'

Japheth took a few steps closer. 'Right, we grab a team that can make the walk. You said it was around five miles out from here?'

Colfer nodded.

'So, we take a team out there to dig. Twelve hours later we will bring out a relief team to take over.' Japheth nodded to himself as he spoke. 'I don't really know how long it takes to dig a hole that big.' Japheth stared into the distance. If they found power, they could live here for years. They would have enough resources to save everyone. And if Japheth took the lead, maybe he could convince the survivors to bring back Alissa, Ham, and Shem. 'Gather the people, Colfer. We need to tell them.'

***

The survivors were grouped together once more looking up to the makeshift stage where Japheth stood front and centre. He had taken the lead while Colfer's voice was just diminishing with every passing minute.

'All right, we've got some work to do today. Seems like we might just have something that could save all our lives.' Japheth paced the stage area as he spoke. 'We need to build shovels, or something similar. Then it's just a short five-mile trek before we start digging in the blazing sun.'

22

The crowd let out a collective groan. They weren't up for this. But they had a good number of strong, capable people, around four hundred. In shifts of a hundred they could have a good rest in between. It took some persuading, but within a few hours, the first team were heading out with Japheth, makeshift shovels slung over their shoulders made from slivers of metallic wall attached to piping with cables. It was rudimentary but it would work.

***

Alissa fell to her knees in the sand. It was still only midmorning, but the sun felt hotter than ever on her skin. Her lips were cracking and crusted with blood. If there was any water left in her body, she might have shed some tears. She just felt like a dried-up husk. Her head was pounding, and the light was blinding her. There was a thick fog where her brain should be, and all she wanted to do was lie in the sand and sleep.

Two sets of arms roughly dragged her back to her feet. With Ham on one side and Shem on the other, they kept moving. *We don't have long now,* Alissa thought.

They walked like that for hours, each of them falling to their knees while the others helped them, but as the midday sun burned their faces, Shem stopped and swung the bag holding the tent from his shoulder and onto the sand. Ham and Alissa helped. The task of setting up the camp had become a three-person job. Eventually they crawled inside and lay on the groundsheet. The temperature was almost unbearable. Alissa lay staring at the canvas ceiling. *This will be the place we die*, she thought over and over again.

Her mind wandered, pulling up memories of the times she spent with Ham and Shem. She thought about her father

23

and his shop. Soon she was delirious, her memories of childhood, meeting Shem, Silver Glove…they all started to blend together as she slowly started to fade away.

'Al, please, wake up.' The voice was faint, but it was pulling her back into the radiant heat of the tent. 'Al, come on, please.' Her eyes opened slowly, and a blurry Shem came into focus above her.

'Thank god, it worked.'

Alissa realised the words were coming from Shem as her mind started to sharpen slightly. 'What's going on, Shem?'

'I was looking through the medi pack. The one Megan gave us. We never thought to look…' His voice trailed off as he lifted his hand. He held three tubes. 'Injectors?'

Alissa wasn't following.

'Isotonic Crystalloid Injectors. They're hydrators.'

Alissa breathed a sigh of relief as she heard Ham murmuring to himself in his sleep.

She lowered her voice. 'We would've died, Shem. How many are there?'

'Just these three.' He dropped the empty tubes to the groundsheet between them.

'How long will they last?' Alissa wasn't sure she wanted the answer.

'If we don't move around too much then forty-eight hours? If we're lucky.'

CHAPTER FOUR

THE JOURNEY TO THE POWER SOURCE ONLY TOOK A few hours of walking. They had stocked up with water and rations and crossed the desert. Japheth was sweating through his shirt by the time they arrived at the location. The team looked to him for instruction, and he stood, staring at them. He had no idea how to deal with people, not really. He shifted uncomfortably as he wordlessly lowered his shovel to the ground.

The sand parted beneath the rough metal, and Japheth swung the shovel over his shoulder, sending grainy particles scattering behind him. He looked at the team as they stared back at him. Within a moment, they jumped into action. The dig began.

Japheth expected a few hours of digging before they were relieved by the second team, but it didn't feel like any time had passed at all. He wasn't ready to go back yet; the manual labour kept his mind from focussing on Alissa, and he relished the peace. He sent the first team back and carried on working with the second.

The hole they had created was around twenty feet in diameter, and he was one of the ones at the bottom when they hit the metal.

'What the Hell?' The voice came from behind him, followed by the clang of metal on metal. Japheth turned quickly and dropped to his knees. Gently, he brushed the sand away to reveal a large metallic panel. It was dotted with low lights flickering along the length of it. It was impossible to tell just how big it was, but he was certain it extended past the confines of their hole. Japheth tapped a knuckle against it. There was a lot of solid metal, but as they dug, they came across what looked like a security panel that sounded hollow when he tapped it.

'Did anyone bring a laser cutter?'

There was some muttering within the group, and the sound of tools being rattled came from outside the hole. A small metal rod with buttons down the side was handed to Japheth. The end was tipped with a sharp-looking needle that glowed white when he pressed the button. Japheth cut through the metal panel, making a large enough space for them to pass through one by one. As he finished the circle of melted slag, the piece fell into the space beneath and hit another metal surface with a bang that echoed through the structure beneath them. Japheth looked at the team then slowly lowered himself in.

As Japheth hung there, gripping the rough metal, he realised he was not alone. He released himself and dropped the last few feet with his hands in the air. In front of him were three human-looking figures, except they had a rather pale green skin tone and slightly too large foreheads that sloped upwards. Their eyes were bigger too and angled wrong. Japheth reasoned, quite correctly, that he was face-to-face with aliens, and they were pointing guns at him.

26

'I'm sorry about the ceiling; we were desperate and looking for power. Please, can you help us?'

The sound that came out of the alien mouths was unlike any language he had heard before. They stepped closer to Japheth and started to search him. He took this opportunity to take in the surroundings. It was a large room, filled with consoles and control panels. They were all lit and functioning well. Clearly this is what their scanners had picked up. One of the aliens grabbed the laser cutter from Japheth's pocket and placed it on the console beside them. They spoke again, looking at their human intruder. The sounds were again jarring to Japheth as he responded, hands still in the air, 'I'm sorry, I don't understand.'

The humanoids looked through the hole above them to see more human faces poking through, staring at the aliens with wide open mouths.

One of them turned back to a panel and began pressing buttons; he then turned to Japheth and in a low voice simply said, 'Speak.'

'Speak what? I don't know what you want me to say.' Japheth's desperate tone echoed as his voice replayed through the room.

The aliens spoke among themselves and turned back to Japheth. 'More.'

It took him a moment to get over the shock of it, but they had just used Earth tongue. If it was some sort of universal translator, it would need lots of samples. 'I am Japheth Riordan by name. I am a human from the planet Earth. Our ship crashed here after it was attacked. We have survivors but we need help.'

The voice echoed around the room again. He could hear his own words, and it was a sad story to tell. One of the aliens stepped forward.

27

'I am Koral by name. I am Drovian from the planet Drovia. Please, you and your people may follow.'

Koral stepped past Japheth and crossed the room to a door on the far side. The rest of the team dropped in one by one. Some were amazed by what they saw, and some were very afraid. They all followed behind Japheth as he crossed the room.

The door was open, and the humans were then led down some rather sketchy-looking hallways. Open metal grating and wiring were on show, like the place was falling to pieces. Japheth took note of what he was seeing and tried to build a mental map. Eventually, after passing through hallways and corridors for about twenty minutes, they stopped at a large double doorway. A few buttons were pressed, and they were shown an amazing view. The doors slid open to reveal a glass walkway. They were around three hundred feet in the air at Japheth's best guess. The space was cavernous, and light shone down onto a huge and really quite beautiful city. The buildings were towering skyscrapers, and he could see parks and people, cars and shops. It was more incredible than anything he had ever seen. He could hear the gasps from the rest of his team and knew they must be thinking the same as he was.

They followed the glass walkway and turned through a door into one of the city towers. They were taken through the building and into a conference room. 'Please, sit.'

The humans did as they were told, and as they rested round the table, the aliens left. A slightly portly man with a bald head and large teeth turned to Japheth. 'What the Hell is going on, man?'

'I don't know.'

'Are these the aliens that shot us out the sky?'

'I don't think so, but I don't know for certain that they weren't involved. This is all as new to me as it is to you.'

'So what do we do? How do we escape?'

Japheth turned to the guy sitting next to him. 'I don't think we're being held against our will.'

'Then let's get out of here!'

'No.' Japheth shook his head. 'There's power here, a full and thriving civilisation. We need their help if we want to survive here.'

Another one of the men piped up. 'What if they don't want to help us? How do we get their power?'

'I don't think we're in a position to force their hand. We just have to hope they want to help us.'

About an hour passed, then the door whooshed open again and three of the pale green aliens entered. They were armed.

Following them into the room was a tall and robed alien. His skin was a darker green and looked remarkably regal alongside his rich purple cloaks. He was followed by a further two-armed men. He walked around the table and took an empty seat in between the talkative, portly human and one of the skinnier, younger men that Japheth had brought.

He looked at the humans with a combination of amusement and confusion. 'You are humans. Yes?'

Japheth nodded. 'Yes, we are. And you are—' He paused for a minute trying to remember. 'Droveran?'

The regal-looking fellow chuckled. 'Drovian, but yes.' He had a thick accent unlike anything Japheth had ever heard, but he was speaking Earth tongue.

'I am Emperor Sorixa. We used technology to listen to you. Our machines translated. Improvements over time.'

Japheth smiled. 'So you understand me?'

The emperor smiled. 'Understand, yes.' He leaned forward. His eyes were kind, and his smile was gentle. 'Tell, how are you here?'

Japheth looked down at his hands. 'We were attacked.' He looked up at the emperor in time to see sadness in his eyes. These aliens were so expressive in their faces. 'It was these creatures from another world that were tall and cruel. With blue skin and heavy brows. They abducted humans and used us to torture our own people.'

The emperor looked horrified. 'What did they do?'

Japheth drummed his fingers gently on the table as he looked around the group. He didn't want to go into it, but the gravity of the situation needed to be made clear. 'They abducted me. Used my image to torture and manipulate a young woman. To turn her into a killer.' He swallowed heavily. 'I was kept in a cell on their ship for years until she found me, saved me.'

The emperor nodded. 'Go on…'

'We escaped their ship and destroyed it in the process. But they had reinforcements close by, and before we knew it, our ship was being blown out of space. We lost thousands in the destruction. Seven hundred. That's all that remains of our people.'

Emperor Sorixa look as though he wanted to cry. 'I am so very sorry for you and your people.' The emperor took the hands of the men beside him and held them in his own while he furrowed his brow and looked deep in thought. The room fell silent until he spoke again. 'Bring your people here. Our city is vast and will offer plenty of space.' He looked up at Japheth. 'It is not our nature to see harm come to those around us. You will be welcomed here by all.'

Japheth rose to his feet and almost ran round the table to Sorixa, who, upon seeing this, stood to face him. Japheth dispensed with formality and wrapped his arms around the emperor, much to the panic of the armed men who reached for their weapons before they heard the emperor chuckle and pull Japheth in closer.

'Come now. Let me show you the city.'

Their grasp of the Earth tongue was improving each time they spoke, and Japheth was impressed at how easy it was to communicate. They were led down through the tower and into the ground level of the underground city.

There they were taken through the city square, an open area with grass and flowers. Japheth looked up at the cavern above them, but instead of seeing a rocky cavern, there was a sky, pale blue with little puffs of white. He stood there, jaw agape as one of the Drovians approached. 'It's not actually sky, you know.' The voice was feminine and gentle. Japheth looked at her as she continued. 'It's actually a radiation screen. Provides us with the vitamins we need from the sun, including the little plants here, but it looks like the real sky.'

'It's amazing.'

'Come on, everyone, keep up,' the emperor called to the humans.

Japheth smiled at the woman and turned back to the group.

The tour continued, past the hospital and the guard house, the shopping centre and the hospitality quarter filled with hotels and restaurants.

The tour ended with the emperor leading them through a door into a hangar bay, filled with small ships and land vehicles.

'Do you need a ride back to your Ark?'

Japheth smiled. 'Thank you, but it's not far. We will return with the others within the day.'

'As you wish.'

With a nod, the guards jumped into action and the huge doors along one wall slid slowly open. Sand fell in a curtain as they fully opened and revealed the desert and allowed the heat to wash over them. The small group of humans began their journey back to the survivors.

***

The journey back took an hour. Along the way there was excited chatter among the group. For the first time since the crash, there was hope and the survivors were clinging onto that. Japheth looked around while they walked, but the hole they dug was nowhere to be seen. The exit was a lot closer to the crash site than the dig site had been.

Colfer spotted the group returning. He had been watching since the first team had returned without Japheth. He didn't trust him; he could still be a plant from the aliens who tried to kill everyone. Maybe it was only a matter of time before he tried it here.

As the group arrived, they started splitting off as Japheth headed to the meeting space they used. Megan arrived at the same time as Colfer, only a few moments after Japheth.

'You might wanna sit down for this.' Japheth smiled, and Megan perched on one of the chairs, holding her bump.

Colfer remained standing. 'Well? What did you find?'

'There's a city under our feet. It's pretty vast down there. I don't know how big it is, but it's beautiful.'

'An abandoned city? That's perfect for us.' Colfer seemed excited by the prospect.

'Actually no. It's not abandoned. There's a race of alien people who live here, the Drovians. They want to welcome us to the city. They say there's enough space for all of us.'

Megan smiled. 'Oh that's wonderful. How long can we stay?'

'Well, it was never officially stated, but I get the feeling we are being offered a permanent home.'

Japheth glanced over at Colfer who had his arms folded and had a smile on his face that more resembled a grimace.

'What's up, Colfer?'

'It just seems to me that the man who was rescued from aliens is now leading us into a city filled with them.' His voice was indignant.

Japheth took a step towards Colfer. There was a flash of anger across his face that made Megan flinch. If Alissa were here, she would say it was the closest Japheth has ever come to resembling Silver Glove. He leaned in close to Colfer. 'You don't ever get to speak about what happened to me. If you don't wanna come with us, then fine. Stay here and rot in the sun.' Japheth turned and stormed away, leaving Colfer wide-eyed and Megan with a look of concern.

It took the humans a few hours to pack up the things they wanted to keep, and Japheth was laughing and joking with a few of the guys he had been to the city with. Megan waddled over to him. He stood up from the crate he was sitting on to greet her.

'You know, medical supply crates aren't designed as chairs.'

Japheth smiled in return. 'They sure are comfy though.'

Things were comfortable between them; Megan enjoyed having a friend through all this. 'Do you think…' Her voice trailed off. 'What I mean is, will there be a way to…'

'You want to save Al.'

'Oh, Japheth, she can't have a lot of time left. None of them can. With the supplies they took, I'd say fifteen hours at the most.'

'We can ask when we get there. I'll get the people to pick up the pace here. See if we can reach the city within the next two hours.'

Megan nodded, and Japheth started ushering people to hurry. It took about fifteen minutes to group everyone up and grab all the things they needed, but then their journey began.

It took longer this time to return to the city. More people meant a slower journey. They eventually arrived at the hangar doors, which had remained open for them. The survivors were brought in and welcomed. During this initial greeting Japheth took Megan by the arm and gently led her to a tall, handsome green-skinned man in purple robes. 'Megan, this is Emperor Sorixa.'

Megan bowed to the man, who chuckled, and Japheth brought her back to standing.

'No need for that here. We are honoured to have you.' He looked her over. 'It seems you are with child. Am I correct?'

Megan nodded. 'Not long now, around two months left.' She patted her bump. 'May I ask you, Emperor, have you found any other humans in the desert? We are missing three of our own.'

'I'm afraid not. However I will send out a few patrols to see if they can be located.'

The next job was Garret. Megan accompanied his pod to the hospital and was given the tour by the doctors there before being shown to where they had stationed Garret within a ward. The pod was fully powered now. It meant the healing process could begin. Megan turned to the young female that had shown her around. 'There were many humans injured in the crash. Do you have the facilities to treat them?'

'No, we have never seen internals like yours before. If you help us, we can amend some of the tools here.'

Megan smiled. 'Looks like I'll have to put off my maternity leave.'

***

The city felt enormous from ground level and yet not oppressive. The people here were friendly. Some stopped Japheth as he walked to ask him about Earth and to see if he liked their city. He did. There was no denying that humanity could be very happy here.

As he walked, he glanced up to the fake sky above and felt the warmth of the projected sun. It was something he had never experienced back home, and it was so different to the harsh sun of the desert. And even though it wasn't real, it felt incredible. Then he saw them. The creatures that took him, they were here, shooting their guns at the innocents. Suddenly people were screaming and running while the sky was destroyed, and thousands of small fighter ships flew in. Japheth stood watching, mouth open, as chunks of rock fell from the sky, crushing the Drovians as they ran. Lasers toppled buildings, and the city was turned the rubble. Japheth stood as the sole survivor of the onslaught. Then everything went black.

***

'Doctor Harper? Could you assist?'

Megan turned to the young nurse. 'Of course, what seems to be the problem?'

'An unconscious human has been brought to us. We do not understand the anatomy enough to heal him.'

With a smile masking her concern, Megan followed the nurse to the other side of the ward where a man was lying on a bed.

'Japheth!' Megan started to check for a pulse. 'What happened?'

'It seems he was walking through the city when he just stopped, started at the sky, then fell to the ground.'

Megan started work on him. Her bag from the Ark had her handheld medical devices, and she began to examine him. 'If I didn't know better, I'd say he was asleep.'

She grabbed a tube from her bag and pressed the needle at the end of it into his arm. It released a liquid into his veins and slowly he began to wake.

'What happened? Where am I?'

'It's all right.' Megan sat on the side of the bed and took his hand. 'What happened out there, Japheth?'

He took a moment, brow furrowed to think. 'There was an attack. I saw it. Thousands of alien ships came and destroyed everything. It felt so real.' His eyes flickered over to the window. Everything looked calm.

'Perhaps you're a Sike.'

Both the humans look over at the pale green nurse as she spoke in a quiet whisper. She immediately looked like she regretted speaking.

'What's a Sike?' Japheth leaned up on his elbows.

'Sometimes Drovians are born with an ability to see things that haven't happened yet.'

'Like a psychic?' Megan chuckled but stopped when she realised she was the only one.

'Sometimes they go their whole lives without ever seeing anything, and sometimes they can do it from childhood.'

The door opened behind her and an armoured guard entered the room. 'Doctor, another human has been located in the desert. Please come with us to offer medical assistance.'

Megan nodded and then glanced over at Japheth. He was already getting off the bed. 'Japheth, you're staying here. You might need treatment.'

He held up a hand to stop her. 'It could be Alissa.'

They hurried back to the same hangar port that they had arrived in. There was a land vehicle, large and sand coloured. It had an open space at the back covered with a canvas for shade. The engine was running, and it was waiting near the open double doors. Japheth climbed in and helped Megan aboard.

They headed out into the desert sands at high speed with sand whipping around them.

'They've been out here a long time, Japheth. I don't know what we're gonna find.' She fiddled with her bag as she spoke. 'Realistically, if they set up a camp, they've got about an hour left, but that's only if they rationed properly and used the hydrators. If they kept pushing on, then we will be way too late.'

Japheth nodded, his jaw set and his brow furrowed as he looked out into the desert. 'I know.'

The view whizzed past but looked unmoving in its vastness. Megan saw, in the distance, a glimmer of something reflecting the hot sun. As they moved in closer, she realised it was their tent. It was Alissa, Ham, and Shem. There was a rush of relief followed by worry.

As they pulled up to the tent, Japheth practically flung himself out of the vehicle and ran to the shelter. One of the Drovians helped Megan down, and she hurried over to the opening. As she reached the tent, Japheth ran out, 'It's Ham. He's alone in there.' His eyes were darting around. 'She wouldn't have gone far from him.' He took off and started searching the area while Megan went inside the tent.

Lying on the floor was Ham. Kneeling beside him, she checked for a pulse. It was weak but it was there. Megan let out a sigh of relief, grabbed a hydrator from her pack, and applied it to his neck. It should keep him stable until they arrived back at the city. 'Okay, he can be moved gently back to the van.'

The guards went in after Megan had exited to lift Ham to safety.

Looking around, she realised quickly that she had lost sight of Japheth.

***

The desert was filled with dunes and dips that he only had to run for a few minutes, and he was already out of sight of the others. He circled the tent, increasing the distance with each rotation. The guards saw and joined in to help. They circled for about ten minutes before he spotted her, lying on her front in the sand, arm outstretched to reach Shem, who was lying on his side.

Japheth called out to the others, and he ran to Alissa's side, dropping to his knees as he reached her. Two more guards arrived as he rolled her onto her back.

'Get him back to Megan, now.' He pointed at Shem, and the guards lifted him and started the short walk back to the truck.

Japheth, red-faced and sweating, gently reached under Alissa and lifted her, holding her close to his chest. He couldn't tell if she was breathing.

He hurriedly made his way back to the van and placed Alissa gently in the open space next to her friends. Megan leaned in and gave Alissa the last hydrator she had brought then turned to Japheth. 'I don't know if we're too late.'

With that, she turned and climbed into the van. Japheth wiped a tear and followed her.

CHAPTER FIVE

ALISSA, HAM, AND SHEM WERE LYING IN ADJACENT BEDS in the ward. Megan finished setting up IVs for them to fully hydrate. Now it was just a matter of time to see if they recovered.

'Doctor Harper?' A voice came from behind her, and she turned to face the ward matron, an older plump woman with very dark green skin. 'You've done enough for them now. You must rest.'

'I can't. I have to make sure they're all right.' Megan turned back and took Alissa's hand. 'We let this happen.'

'You've been working for thirteen hours. Maybe the matron is right.' Japheth spoke calmly from the chair beside Ham's bed.

'I used to work thirty-hour shifts back on Earth.'

The matron placed a hand on her shoulder. 'Yes, but you didn't carry life in you back then, am I correct?'

Megan's shoulders slumped. The matron was right. She kept getting so caught up in the people around her that she put her own comfort and the safety of her child to the side.

'Fine, I'll go.' She turned to leave but stopped at the doorway. 'If they wake up…'

'I'll call you straight away,' Japheth reassured her and Megan left the ward.

Her room in the hospitality quarter was nice. There was plenty of space—two bedrooms and a nice kitchen area with real food included. In a better mood, this place would've been like heaven.

Clarke would have loved this.

Hot tears fell down her cheeks. She held it together for everyone else, but she wished with every beat of her heart that Clarke was still here. She cradled her bump, the only part of him that would survive, and she wept for the life they could've had together. She thought about the lazy Sunday mornings when Clarke would cook breakfast. Megan had always wanted two children, a full perfect little family. The children giggling and playing while she drank coffee and watched Clarke make pancakes.

Megan made her way to the bed, lay down, and cried herself to sleep.

***

Alissa felt dry. Her lips were cracked and sore, and she couldn't remember going back to the tent. But there was no sand under her. She opened her eyes and saw bright lights above her. They hurt her head. She was definitely in a bed. She started to sit up, and she saw a person, but not a person. They had green skin, and their face wasn't quite right.

Alien.

Alissa felt the adrenaline pump through her body, and she leapt out of the bed onto her feet, yanking the IV stand

42

and sending it toppling to the ground, shattering its glass bottle. She pulled the wires from her hand, and her eyes searched the room. Ham and Shem were in the beds beside her, there was the one alien, and—she had to look twice—Japheth. He was running towards her, arms reaching for her. Alissa reacted without thinking and threw herself at him, wrapping her arms around his neck as he held her close.

'Where are we?' She released him and looked around the room.

'Well, the short version is that this is an alien civilisation living under the planet we crashed into.' Japheth looked her over. 'Are you all right? It was close, Alissa. We almost lost all of you.'

'I feel okay, but clearly I've missed a lot.' she tried to swallow, but her throat felt like sandpaper. 'I could use some water.'

Japheth nodded. 'I'll take care of it.' As he moved away, the green-skinned nurse gingerly stepped closer. 'Come, sit back down.'

Alissa looked sheepishly around at the mess on the floor. 'I'm sorry, I just…'

'It's all right. You were afraid. Don't worry. We are here to help you heal.'

Japheth returned carrying a glass of water. As he handed it to Alissa, she grabbed it and desperately swallowed it all.

'Well, I was gonna say sip it…'

Alissa smiled. 'I needed that.'

Japheth took Alissa's hand in his own. 'You up for a walk?'

Alissa looked to the nurse. 'Don't go far, but you're all right to take a short break.'

Japheth led her from the room by the hand and gently helped her down to the city. Along the way he pointed out of

43

the hospital windows at buildings he now recognised—the guard house, the library, the hospitality quarter. Alissa followed him, still holding his hand, in silence.

Once they reached the ground floor they walked out into the open city and Alissa stood, mouth hanging open, watching the aliens walk around her. Her body tensed, ready to fight, until she heard Japheth's gentle voice. 'It's all right Alissa. I'm here. You can be calm.'

She was instantly transported back to the facility and Silver Glove's sweet tone as he manipulated her into almost committing murder. For a split second she considered running until her senses came back to her and she felt in her hand, not a silver glove, but another hand made of flesh and bone.

He's not Silver Glove.

Alissa repeated the words in her mind as Japheth continued their walk. He led her to a small grassy area and sat himself down against a tree. Alissa sat cross-legged on the grass facing him.

'Alissa, these people, they have offered us sanctuary within their home, offered us protection from the committee. They see us as refugees of war and want to protect the last of humanity. I don't know how long this will last, but all we need is some time to regroup and figure out where our journey takes us next.'

'I really missed you.'

Japheth's eyes widened. There was a look of confusion on his face. 'Where did that come from?'

Alissa blushed slightly. 'I just—' She paused and took a deep breath. 'I've spent so much time with you, and the other you...You're in my head. Without you there, I felt lonely.'

44

Japheth smiled and took her hand. 'I feel it too…' His voice trailed off, and the two sat there, holding hands in a comfortable silence.

'What happened to Garret?'

'He's still unconscious, but healing. Megan thinks he's going to recover.'

Alissa nodded before she stood back up, releasing Japheth's hand from her own. 'I have to get back to the hospital; I need to be there when Ham and Shem wake up.'

Japheth nodded. 'I'll walk you back.'

***

The ward was still quiet when they arrived. The nurse implied that it was very early in the morning still. They were technically not on the full-day shift yet. Alissa sat herself in a chair between Ham and Shem while Japheth settled at the other side of the room. Shem woke up first and sat up in the bed. He saw Alissa and visibly relaxed. 'Al? What's going on?'

Alissa started to explain while Ham woke up and she went back over the story again. Japheth interrupted a few times with more detail, and each time he did Shem scowled his way. Alissa wasn't blind to this, but what could she say?

While the discussion was underway, a nurse came into the room and pressed some buttons on one of the screens on the wall. It flashed to life, and the emperor's face filled it. Japheth whispered who the alien was for the benefit of the three. The nurse smiled.

'Good morning, my family,' the emperor began. 'It is with great pleasure I welcome the newest members of the Drovian society, the humans.'

The nurse began to clap and looked at the four humans in the room. Alissa smiled shyly, which was a new look for her, one that both Japheth and Shem noticed.

'It seems that they will be with us for a considerable amount of time, so after much deliberation with our council, we have decided to offer the humans permanent residence in our home.'

The emperor paused to let the new announcement sink in. Once he began again, he had a beaming smile. 'We can learn a great deal from the humans with their technological knowledge. And we can share our own with them. This is an opportunity for an even greater civilisation to grow from the choices we make today. I urge each of you to spend time with our new family, welcome them, and help them become productive members of our society.'

The screen went blank, and the nurse turned to the four humans again. 'Welcome to our home. I hope you are as happy as I am to have you here.'

With a smile, she turned and left the room.

Shem rose to his feet. 'What the Hell? They just welcome a bunch of aliens into their city. Are they insane? Is this a trick?'

Alissa shook her head. 'I don't know. Japheth made the first contact with them.'

Shem rolled his eyes and looked over at his rival. 'Well?'

'Well, it seems that due to our gentle nature as a people and the efforts some have already made in sharing knowledge and helping the city, they deem us fit to share their home. It's not unreasonable, after all. Their only alternative is to throw us back out into the desert.'

As he spoke, the nurse came back in. 'Temperatures, everyone.' The nurse walked to each patient in turn, taking their temperatures and comparing to a data pad in her hand.

Alissa turned back to Japheth. 'The desert is the worst place we could be right now. Even if we had supplies and power, we wouldn't last long.'

'You're right. With the Committee after us, we'd be an open target up there,' he replied.

The nurse squealed and her eyes widened. The four humans looked at her as she backed away. As soon as she was close to the door, she turned and ran.

'I guess these guys have heard of our old friends.' Shem nodded towards the door as he spoke.

'Which means the Committee is a well-known entity out there.' Japheth sighed. 'Maybe living here won't be so bad. The people are nice, and the city is beautiful. We could make a home here.' While he spoke, he glanced over at Alissa, a glance that she didn't notice. But Shem did.

'Right,' Alissa said as she stood up. 'I'm going to see Garrett.'

CHAPTER SIX

ALISSA GOT DIRECTIONS TO GARRET'S ROOM FROM ONE   of the women behind a desk. It was a short journey, only a few minutes. She walked into the room and looked at Garrett. He was still in the pod, and she gently rested her hand on the clear glass.

'We're safe, Garrett.'

She sat there for about an hour in silence, a repeat of her behaviour on the surface. She willed him to wake up.

'Alissa?'

The voice came from behind her. With superior reflexes, Alissa leapt to her feet and spun to face the door. It was Megan. Alissa practically flew the few steps across the room and wrapped Megan in a gentle but warm hug. It was slightly more difficult to navigate around the bump, but it worked.

'Al, hun, you're gonna have to let me go.' The muffled voice of the doctor interrupted the embrace, and Alissa released her grasp.

'Sorry, I'm just so happy to see you.'

'Me too, Al. Truth is, I thought you would've died before we found you.'

Alissa furrowed her brow. 'We should have. But you saved our lives.'

Now it was Megan's turn to look confused. 'I did?'

'The hydrators. We found them at just the right time. They gave us an extra day we shouldn't have had.'

Megan's eyes welled up, and she glanced down at Garrett. 'He's going to be okay, Al.'

Alissa followed the doctor's gaze back to the pod.

'He's coming out of the pod tomorrow. It's amazing; he's just getting stronger every day. We're going to wake him up in a few days if he doesn't manage it on his own.'

***

After a few hours of flitting around the hospital, Ham, Shem, and Alissa were officially discharged. Japheth offered to escort them to the hospitality quarter, and the quartet reached the city level. As they did, a few of the armed guards approached them. Alissa tensed, ready to fight if needed, but the guards ignored her completely. Instead, they went straight to Japheth.

'We need you to come with us, now.'

Alissa watched as Japheth inspected each one before answering, 'All right. But my companions will need to be shown to the hospitality quarter.'

'That can be taken care of.' The men escorted Japheth down the pavement while one of the men remained behind.

Alissa tried to get past him. 'Wait, Japheth! Where are you taking him?'

'That's confidential information. Please come with me.'

'No! Japheth, what's going on?'

He turned his head to look at Alissa. 'I don't know. Go with your friends. I'll be all right.'

With outstretched arms, a guard ushered the three friends along the pathway and to the hospitality quarter.

It was a beautiful place, a small section of the city with towering hotels, gorgeous parks, eateries, and entertainment. Alissa spotted some of the survivors milling around, including Daniel Colfer. He was sitting outside a restaurant sipping something out of a big white cup, chatting with a few of the other survivors.

While she stared, she heard Shem's voice. 'Thanks for the escort, but I think we can take it from here.'

'No problem.'

Alissa hadn't taken her eyes off Colfer.

'Hey, Al? You okay?'

'He banished us, Shem. He sent us out there to die. He sent Ham…' Her voice trailed off.

'It's okay, Alissa. I'm okay, see?' Ham put his hand on her arm, and she turned to face him. He looked terrified and she realised how wild she must look.

'I'm sorry, Ham.' She leaned against him while he hugged her.

Shem shuffled uncomfortably. 'Come on, let's just go inside and get settled.'

As the three friends walked into the hotel, Japheth was being escorted into what looked like an interrogation room. They sat him down at a table, and one of the guards stood beside the door with his gun in his hands. Japheth frowned. There was no explanation for this, unless they knew about Silver Glove. That might be difficult to explain.

A few minutes passed and two men walked in. Both well dressed in suits. Sitting opposite Japheth, one placed a data slate on the table and pressed a few keys, 'Interview begins.' He leaned back in his chair and looked at Japheth.

'You know why you're here?'

'No.'

The alien nodded. 'All right.' The man sitting next to him shuffled some papers out of a file and handed them to the interviewer. He glanced over them. 'We had a report. One of the nurses in the hospital heard you talk about the Committee. Is that true?'

'Well, yes. Is that a crime?'

'Not ordinarily, but the Committee is made up of many alien races. We want to ensure you're not a part of it.'

Japheth laughed. 'Are you kidding me?' He jumped to his feet, voice raised. 'Are you kidding me! They tortured me! They used me. They tried to kill me and the entire human race! I am absolutely not a part of it!'

It wasn't often that Japheth lost his temper, and it was enough for the guard to aim his gun at him. The interviewer raised his hands. 'All right, sit down, sir, or you're going to get shot.'

Japheth looked around to see the guard prepared to shoot and slumped back down into the chair.

'I'm not part of it.'

'Tell me more about what happened to you.'

Japheth recounted the most recent years of his life in that interrogation room. He told them about being abducted, about being used as part of the hologram technology, about Silver Glove and Alissa, the Ark, the prison ship, and the fall. Hours passed while he talked, careful not to leave anything out.

'Tell me about the vision.'

Japheth looked blankly at him. 'What vision?'

'The nurse told us—you had a vision of war.'

'Yeah, I guess so. I mean, I saw ships. Thousands of them attacking the city and killing everyone. I don't know how it happened, but the nurse said I'm a Sike.'

The interviewer raised an eyebrow and made some notes in the file. 'Interesting, what do you know about Sikes?'

Japheth shook his head. 'Nothing. I know nothing.'

'A Sike is a being that through birth or trauma is given access to a higher plane of thought.' The interviewer shuffled in his seat slightly as he handed some of the paperwork he was writing on to the armed guard. He in turn took it and left the room.

'Some folks believe a Sike can see the future. But they're the type to believe in magic and all that nonsense. It is more likely that the Sike can interpret all available information and process it, creating a vision so the brain can comprehend what it's understood on a subconscious level.'

Japheth rubbed his hands over his face and chuckled slightly. 'So, all the fiddling round with my brain and they made me psychic?' He laughed again. 'It's just…insane.'

The interviewer stood up. 'Hmm yeah, insane,' he mumbled to himself as he left Japheth alone in the room.

***

Alissa sat on quite a squishy bed. It was certainly the most comfortable bed she had felt in a long time, maybe ever. Ham sat beside her, and Shem took the armchair across the room. He turned it to face the window and stared out at the city.

'Hey, Al, are we gonna live here forever now?' Ham leaned himself against the wall.

'It seems likely. I mean, The Ark was supposed to find a planet to colonise. There was nothing that said the planet has to be empty, I guess.'

Ham nodded as she spoke. 'I do like it here. The people are nice, and it's cleaner than New Amerland.'

New Amerland. It seemed like a lifetime ago for Alissa. Clanging around with her anti grav boots, fixing ships, and drinking in Saime's Bar. Or being kidnapped tortured and nearly killed. Her memories of both were just as vivid.

'Probably no murderous holograms here either,' Shem muttered. His mood seemed better in the hospital but since they arrived at the hotel, he had just seemed mad.

'Shem, what's the matter with you?' Alissa tried very carefully to keep her voice gentle and light.

'What? Oh, nothing.'

Alissa sat quietly and watched as Shem continued to stare out of the window.

The three of them had been given one big apartment to share. They couldn't tell them how long this would be for, but Alissa didn't care. She was just happy to be safe with Ham and Shem. The space they were given was quite luxurious. It had one large room with seating and a table when you first walked in with four doors along the walls. Three were bedrooms and one was a bathroom. Alissa had never had this much space, and even better, she was sharing it with her friends. And there was no responsibility now. Alissa was free to just relax and enjoy her life here, which was a luxury she thought would never be awarded to her.

***

Japheth sat staring at the wall of the interrogation room. It felt like centuries had passed and he had been forgotten about. He leaned forward over the metal table and rested his head on his arms. His eyes felt heavy and began to close as the door swung open.

It was Emperor Sorixa. He walked into the room and sat down. 'Hello again, Japheth.'

'You really deal with a lot of things personally, don't you?'

The emperor tilted his head. 'Of course, these are my people.'

Japheth sat back in the chair. 'So, are we going to discuss my arrest and subsequent interrogation?'

'You haven't been arrested. You've been temporarily detained while we understand the extent of your relationship with the Committee.'

Japheth leaned forward. 'I don't have a relationship with the Committee.'

'But they abducted you, used your brain, and even implanted chips in there. Like it or not, the committee was responsible for everything that happened to you. I would say that's a pretty intense relationship.'

Japheth looked down at the table. 'Yes, well. I don't exactly look back on those memories fondly.'

'I know. And that is the reason you're not currently locked in a cell for the rest of your life. Instead, you and I are talking.' Emperor Sorixa rose gracefully to his feet and began to pace the room. 'Centuries ago, we were land dwellers, with the technology and the drive to visit the stars. Many were sent exploring, and many were lost. It seemed there was a presence ready to destroy us if we left our own system. Eventually they attacked the planet. They rained fire down on us, and the streets ran red with the blood of our families. Some of us escaped into SEF, a corporation that manufactured space technology and ships. We hollowed the place out and eventually created the city you look upon now. Others around the planet did the same.'

The emperor wiped a tear from his cheek and continued. 'They blasted the surface until there was nothing left, nothing but dust. Then they left. They believed we were extinct; they had no idea we had survived. Not only that, but we learned to thrive down here. This became our civilisation, our home, and our way of life. But now, you've led them back here, and they will be looking for you. You're going to lead the Committee to our front door.'

Japheth looked up at the emperor. 'I'm sorry. I'm so sorry.'

Emperor Sorixa nodded. 'I know. And truth be told, this is no fault of yours. You cannot be blamed for suffering the same fate as our ancestors.' He turned to Japheth. 'You are no prisoner here. You're free to leave.' And with those words, the emperor left the room.

***

The fake sky was getting dim, and Alissa wanted something sweet to finish the day for comfort. She left her bedroom, which was now empty of people as Ham and Shem had since moved to their own. She crossed the living space and left the room.

It was a short walk to the turbo lifts that took her to the city level below. There were still people milling around, humans and drovians making friends and getting to know one another. Alissa smiled. She liked seeing her people happy and relaxed. While staring at two young Drovian children chasing one of the engine techs from the Ark, giggling as they ran, Alissa walked straight into someone and toppled backwards. A hand came down to help her, so Alissa took it and looked at the owner. 'Colfer?'

He pulled her to her feet. 'Hi, Alissa.'

They stood there in silence both staring at each other, until Alissa cut right to the chase. 'Are you going to apologise for trying to kill me Ham and Shem?'

'Are you going to apologise for chasing aliens and getting thousands of people killed?'

She stepped backwards. 'I thought you would've been there to introduce us to the emperor. After all, you're supposed to be leading our people, aren't you?'

She pushed past him with her shoulder and let her words sink in. If nothing else, the satisfaction of that conversation would keep her going for weeks.

With her heart pounding, she ran back up to her room empty-handed. When she arrived, Shem was sitting at the table in the living space. She greeted him and headed towards her room, but he stopped her and asked her to sit with him at the table. She did as she was asked.

'What's up, Shem?'

'I need you to move out.'

Alissa felt like she had just been punched in the stomach. 'What? Why?'

Shem didn't look up from the table. 'You know why.'

'No, I don't.' Her voice was pleading.

He still didn't look up.

'I love you, Al. But I can't keep being punished for that.'

'I'm not—I'm not punishing you, I...' Her voice trailed off.

'I know you want to love me. But you can't, because of him. He has you in a way I never will. So, I need you to move out.'

Alissa let the tears fall down her cheeks as Shem stood up. He walked around the table and squeezed her shoulder before walking back to his room.

This was too much. Why did Shem get to be the calm guy while she was acting like an emotional wreck?

***

The evening was still early when Japheth arrived back at the hospitality quarter. The officers had offered him a position with them—street guard. It was nothing special to anyone else, but for him, it was a taste of normality that had been out of his grasp for so long, a chance to live a life free of torture and pain. It was during this thought that he turned the corner and saw Alissa. Her shoulders were hunched over, and her hands were stuffed into her pockets as she walked. 'Alissa?'

She looked up at him. 'Hey, are you all right? What happened with the guards?' Her face was tear-streaked and her eyes were puffy.

Japheth wrapped her up in his arms. He loved the feel of her as she reciprocated the hug. 'I'm all right. It was nothing. Why are you crying?'

Alissa sniffed and wiped her face with her hands. 'Forget it. I'm fine.'

Japheth released her from his embrace. 'All right. Would you like me to walk you back to your room?'

Alissa started crying again. 'I can't go back there.'

'Why not?'

'Because Shem kicked me out.' Fresh tears fell down her cheeks, and she tried to hide them with her hand.

'He's obviously gone insane. Come on, I'll take care of this.' He took her by the hand and started leading her back to her hotel.

'No! Seeing us together is only gonna upset him more.'

Japheth stopped pulling and looked her over with his brow furrowed. 'Then where would you like me to take you?'

They stood silently on the path, Japheth still holding her hand and eyeing her carefully as she thought. 'Maybe, we could just get coffee or something?'

'I think that's a great idea.' Japheth smiled gently.

He didn't let go of her hand. Instead, he walked by her side as they navigated the hospitality sector to a small coffee shop. There they found a table on the patio and looked out at the city as they drank hot beverages. It was similar to coffee, at least, the coffee Alissa had on The Ark. The stuff back in New Amerland was considerably weaker. This had a flavour that was quite robust. She liked it.

The two sat in silence for a while, neither wanting to be the first to speak. Alissa felt embarrassed for her tears over Shem, and it seemed Japheth didn't want to look her in the eye. She stared at the steam coming from the cup and forced fresh tears not to fall. The café they were in was getting quieter as the early evening wore on. Alissa still eyed up her coffee. The steam had dissipated as the drink cooled and now she was staring at a lukewarm cup.

'Do you think the silence has gone on long enough?' Japheth was looking at her now. Something he had avoided for the last hour. 'Or do you want to carry on awkwardly? Because honestly, I don't mind. I'd just rather know either way.'

Alissa let out a slight chuckle and looked across at Japheth. He still had the face of a torturer. The face of evil.

But there was such kindness behind his eyes. Alissa knew none of her feelings were his fault, the fear and hatred that bubbled deep inside when she saw him out the corner of her eye. Every time they spoke, her heart fluttered with excitement while bile rose in her throat from the memory of the dagger sliding into her belly. She hated the duplicity of it and tried to hide it from Japheth. It wasn't his fault.

'I think I should see if Megan is home. Maybe I can stay with her?' Alissa was thinking out loud, but Japheth seemed relieved that she had joined the conversation.

'Not a bad idea. She's getting bigger every day. I'll bet she could use help around the place.'

They sat for another half hour before Japheth shifted in his seat a little uncomfortably. 'What did you mean before, Alissa?'

She looked at him. 'When?'

'Earlier, you said seeing us together is only going to upset Shem more.' Japheth shifted again.

'Shem is in love with me.'

Japheth smiled. 'He's made that quite clear.'

'Yeah, I know.'

'Do you love him?'

Alissa took a moment to think. 'I think I did. Back in New Amerland, before the Facility and The Ark.' She sighed heavily. 'It's just…so much has changed, I don't know how I feel anymore. But he thinks I'm in love with you.'

'Are you?' There was hope in his voice.

Alissa took his hand and stared at it while she squeezed it gently. 'I don't…I don't know.'

Japheth looked down while she carried on.

'It's just that, to me there will always be a part of my mind that sees you as Silver Glove. That'll never go away.

And yet, there were all those nights where I dreamed of you…'

'I get it.' Japheth's voice was gentle.

'I'm not sure that you do. I've known Shem for years, and I've always known how he felt about me. But I always felt like there was something stopping me from taking that step with him.'

Japheth looked back up at Alissa. Her eyes were glistening as she spoke. 'Then there was Silver Glove. A man so intoxicating I was willing to kill for him. I let him manipulate me in a way I've never experienced before. I'm scared to let myself feel that way about you.' Japheth shifted uncomfortably as she continued. 'I'm scared of the power you would have over me.'

Japheth stood up and held out his hand for Alissa to take. Once she had, he pulled her to her feet and into a tight hug and spoke quietly into her ear. 'I'll never hurt you, Al.'

Alissa smiled into his shoulder as her held her. 'I'm gonna hold you to that.'

Japheth gently let go and allowed his hand to slip into hers. 'Come on. Let's get you to Megan's.'

As he led her through the hospitality quarter, he held her hand. It felt uncomplicated. Like her hand was made for his. Alissa tried to think about other things, but she couldn't help but let her mind wander to Japheth. It felt electric.

CHAPTER SEVEN

SHEM WOKE UP EARLY AS USUAL, STRETCHED, AND GOT out of bed. Last night he had his heart broken for the last time, and he actually felt free. He had finally taken control of the situation, made it clear that Al no longer had the choice. Being with Shem was off the table.

He walked into the communal area and saw Ham sitting at the table. He looked upset.

'What's up, Ham?' Shem asked as he walked over to the table and sat down.

'Alissa didn't come home last night. And I don't know where she is so I can't message her.'

'It's okay, Ham. I asked her to leave.'

Ham looked betrayed. 'What? Why would you do that?'

'Honestly, being around her was killing me. She can't love me back, and I can't stop loving her.' Shem's eyes watered.

It was very rare that Ham saw Shem this way, but he couldn't see past this. 'How could you? She's our best friend, my best friend.' Ham started heading back to his room. 'I know I'm not that smart, but I understand her. She needs us now more than she ever has before, and all you can think about is yourself. You're being an idiot.'

'I know, Ham, but I—'

Ham cut him off. 'It's not about you, Shem.'

***

It became quickly apparent that life within this underground city would closely resemble life within the complexes back on Earth. Alissa pondered this while sitting on the kerbside outside the hospitality district. It had been a week since she had left the apartment she was sharing with Ham and Shem. Megan had taken her in with open arms. It felt nice to have some distance from Shem and she understood now what she couldn't fathom before. Shem would never stop loving her as long as she was around him every day. He needed time to move on, to discover who he wanted to be in this new life. Alissa hoped very much that they would eventually reconnect, but that would come down to him. It would also depend on Japheth. She hadn't seen him face-to-face since the night he walked her to Megan's. It was clear to her that, much like Shem, she needed distance to understand her own feelings. There was an aura around Japheth that she couldn't resist, but if she fell down the rabbit hole with him, especially so soon, it would destroy Shem completely and irreparably ruin their friendship.

While she was lost in thought, one of the small motor vehicles had broken down. Alissa smiled and let her inner mechanic out.

'Anything I can help with?' She smiled at the drovian man.

'Depends, can you fix these things?' He looked dubious. After all, Alissa was a human, their tech was vastly different in a lot of ways.

After a few more moments of awkward conversation with the alien owner, Alissa was shoulder deep in the vehicle internal workings. The engines were designed in a totally alien way—but they weren't too dissimilar to the essential engine functions when you broke them down into their component parts. She felt a presence lower itself beside her while she held an engine part in one hand and a laser screwdriver in the other. With a quick side glance, she realised it was Ham and smiled. 'Hey, big guy, where have you been hiding, huh?'

Ham peered into the open panel on the side of the vehicle while he answered, 'I've been around. It's you that vanished.' He pointed into the hole. 'That piece there, it's burned out.' He reached in, gently disconnected it, and handed it to Alissa. 'I can rewire around it as a temporary fix, but it's gonna need a new part.'

Alissa smiled and looked up at the driver who had been pacing anxiously. 'You hear that? You're gonna be all right. Just a replacement thingy.' She held up the part as the engine whirred back to life. 'Done.'

Ham smiled and helped Alissa to her feet. She handed the burned-out part to the driver, and he thanked them before hopping back into his little runner and heading down the road.

Alissa watched him drive away for a few minutes before turning back to Ham. 'So, how's life been treating you?'

She barely got the words out before Ham wrapped her in the biggest hug and lifted her from the ground. 'I've missed you so much.'

'I've missed you too, Ham. But it's only been a week since I left the apartment.' Her reply was muffled by his frame, and he gently put her down and smiled shyly at the floor.

'Shem misses you too.'

It was Alissa's turn to look away. 'I know. But you get why he needs me to stay away, right?'

'I guess.' Ham shifted uncomfortably. 'But why do I get punished?'

Alissa felt a pang of guilt, she should be making more of an effort with Ham. 'Tell you what, why don't we go to the food court and just eat all day?' She took hold of his hand. 'We have a ton of catching up to do, Ham. I want to know everything you've been doing.'

She smiled as she led her friend by the hand to the dining quarter.

***

The room was mostly dark, gently lit by blue-tinted lights that ran along the floor. They were dim but cast large shadows. The edge of his vision was blurred. He was in a place he didn't recognise. He was on a bed, that much he could tell, but where?

Garret struggled to cast his mind back. What was the last thing he remembered? There was an alien ship? That couldn't be right.

He shook his head. It was right. There were aliens. Or at least a ship. It fired on them. Garrett groaned and reached his hands up to his face. The Ark, they destroyed it. They blew it to smithereens.

But if that's true? How am I alive?

Do the aliens have him now? Is he their prisoner?

The old man tried to pull himself into a more upright position, groaning as he manoeuvred his arms and crying out in pain as he tried to push himself up. With a frustrated sigh, he relaxed his muscles as a door slid open across the room. Garret's eyes flickered over to the opening and widened when he saw the tall creature with pale green skin walk into the room. 'No!' He tried to move, but he was weak.

The alien approached and smiled. 'Mr. Garret, you're awake!'

He nodded, open-mouthed at the question.

'Excellent.' The creature turned to leave. 'I will alert the human doctor.'

The alien left, and after only a few minutes, the door opened once more and Megan ran into the room. 'Garret!' She hurried to his bedside. 'You're alive! Thank God. I've been so worried.'

Garret finally found his words. 'What the Hell is going on?'

'It's a long story, but I'll do my best. I'm gonna call Alissa too. She's been worried.'

It took half an hour for Alissa to arrive. In that time, Megan had run extensive tests on Garret while she told him about the alien community and how they had been welcomed as guests. She looked at the computer while she talked, 'Realistically, you should be dead, Garret.'

He nodded, and she continued, 'You have a few internal bumps and bruises left, but this technology will have you back on your feet again in no time.'

'On my feet again to do what, exactly?'

Megan looked at him and smiled weakly. 'I know life is gonna look different for us now…but we have to make the best of it.' Her hand rested instinctively on her baby bump.

Garret's eyes widened as if he'd only just noticed. 'Megan...you're both...okay?' His eyes flitted between the bump and her face while Megan just smiled sadly and nodded.

With perfect timing, the door opened and Alissa stepped through. Upon seeing Garret, she hurried to his side and wrapped her arms around his neck. Suddenly tears sprang from her eyes and she sobbed into his shoulder while he held her protectively.

He graciously gave her a few moments before he spoke. 'Miss Namaah? You have rather a tight grip.'

Alissa's eyes widened, and she let go of him instantly. 'Oh god, I'm sorry! I just...I didn't think you would ever wake up.' She looked down at her hands. 'It's been kinda rough here.'

'So, I've heard.' He glanced up to Megan, who smiled at Alissa. 'I told him about the crash and how Japheth found this place and the aliens here.'

Alissa nodded. Megan hadn't mentioned Colfer or Alissa's banishment to Garret. She assumed it was to protect Colfer. Not that it mattered now. Their commander was awake, and all responsibility fell with him. Alissa felt the weight of the world lift off her shoulders, and her eyes welled up again.

CHAPTER EIGHT

COLFER WALKED THROUGH THE BUSTLING STREETS OF   the alien city, completely surrounded by moving bodies yet utterly alone. The citizens of Earth barely spoke to him, which cut him deeply. Considering they still fawned over the girl who almost got them all killed.

He hated Alissa. Hated her because she was brave enough to sacrifice everything for what she believed in. But had he not done the same? He banished her to protect the survivors. But that's not why people hated him. It was the fact he banished the idiot as well—that's what bothered people. But Ham had decided to join them on their mission, to infiltrate an alien ship to save a man no one knew.

Perhaps he was misled by Alissa and Shem, but that doesn't mean Ham should be free from punishment. The survivors put Colfer in charge, and now, suddenly, they all wanted to follow this Japheth man, the one that tortured humans and worked with aliens. How could they be certain that he was free from alien control? Colfer shook his head as he walked, barely taking in the scenery around him as it changed from city to more green areas before eventually petering out into rocky shale and dust. He had reached the limits of the civilisation. Dejectedly, he sat on the dusty ground and lost himself in deep thought.

***

'So…you were banished from the survivor camp by Daniel Colfer?' Alissa nodded in response and looked at the ground. 'I'm not a very good leader, Garret. He was right to punish me.'

Garret took in a deep breath and rested a hand gently on her shoulder. 'Alissa—'

He paused. The annoying habit was still very much a part of him, and for once, Alissa appreciated it. She sat quietly as he continued.

'I didn't make you into the security chief because of your immaculate leadership skills. You're inexperienced, obsessed with your own problems, and easily distracted.'

The words were harsh and stung, but they were true.

'I made you into the chief so we could carry out a mission we thought was right.'

Megan shifted uncomfortably when Garret brought up the mission to kill the captain.

'You were told to kill someone to save The Ark…but…you didn't do it. You let Clarke Andover talk, you listened, and you gave up any chance you had to get freedom from our dying home.'

Alissa looked at Garret. He looked so old. She had never really noticed that before.

'You were willing to die to protect someone you didn't even know. That's who you are, Alissa. You risked

68

everything to help free Japheth.' Garret sifted slightly while he spoke and winced. Alissa frowned.

'Maybe I should let you get some rest.' Garret shook his head in response, 'Your protective nature shines through in everything you do. This isn't about being a good leader. You are the mother to this crew. Willing to give up everything to save them.'

Tears were falling freely, and Alissa reached up to wipe them away. Megan sat down beside her and wrapped an arm around her shoulder. The three of them sat in silence for a few moments until Garret slowly stood up, leaning painfully onto a dark brown cane. It was beautifully carved and gifted to him by the hospital. Megan had told him that while they were able to mostly repair the damage to his body, his knees were likely to cause him difficulty for the rest of his days. He accepted his fate. He was an old man. He might as well act like it.

He walked over to the window and looked out over the city below. 'I want to speak with the emperor.' He turned back to where Alissa sat. 'What was his name?'

'Sorixa.'

Garret nodded again and looked out over the city once more. 'And Japheth. You say he made the first contact with the people here?'

Megan nodded.

'All right. Bring him in. Call Colfer as well. I want to discuss his actions.'

***

As Colfer sat in the dust, he let his mind wander. He remembered the faces of the friends he lost in the crash, saw the flames lick at the bodies crumpled along the carpeted

69

hallways of The Ark as it fell from the sky. He remembered thinking this was it; this was how he was going to die. He faced his mortality that day, and he let it consume him.

He thought about the day he watched Alissa bare her soul to some seven hundred survivors. He watched as she explained her actions. The pieces fell together in his head, and all the loss and the hurt fell at her feet. She was responsible.

He sat in silence, his mind whirling when there was a ringing coming from his pants pocket. He frowned for a moment before remembering the communicator devices the aliens had provided for them. He pulled it free of the fabric and looked down at it. There was nothing special about it. In fact, it was quite simple compared to the comms systems they used on The Ark, but it did have vocal, text, and recording capabilities. He sighed and answered it.

'Colfer?'

He didn't immediately recognise the voice. 'Who is this?' he asked.

'It's Megan. Listen, Garret is awake, and he wants to see you. Please come to City Hall.'

Colfer felt the blood drain from his face, but he kept his voice from wavering. 'When?'

'Now, Colfer.'

The comms went dead, and he slowly dragged himself to his feet and trudged back towards the city.

***

Emperor Sorixa sat in a large plush seat at the head of the conference table. Behind him was a huge window with an amazing view of the city. His clasped hands rested upon the glass surface of the table, with a cup of warm liquid resting beside them. With a smile, he rose to his feet as Garret entered the room, followed by Alissa and Megan.

'Pleased to meet you, Commander.' The emperor smiled as Garret limped into the room. 'Please sit down and rest your legs.'

Garret gratefully accepted the invitation and placed the cane against the table beside him.

Alissa stood protectively beside Garret as Megan eased herself into the next chair. The emperor sat back down and smiled once more at his guests. 'I was pleased to hear you had awoken.'

Garret nodded and smiled curtly. 'Many expected I would not, it seems.'

Sorixa tilted his head. 'Perhaps, but surely they are satisfied by this outcome?'

A puzzled look crossed Garret's face as he listened to the emperor speak. It was like hearing a thesaurus hold a conversation. Megan had explained about the universal translators and how they would take time to work. The strange vocal characteristics actually amused Garret. He allowed the pleasant feeling to surface in a genuine smile. 'They are indeed satisfied,' he responded.

'Should we commence with the meeting?'

'We are just waiting for one more person.'

Japheth rushed through the city after receiving the comms message. He honestly felt like his part in all this political stuff was over. But somehow he kept getting dragged in. He turned the corner towards City Hall and spotted Colfer just heading into the building. With a frown, he followed close behind. Had they invited him to the meeting as well? Japheth rolled his eyes at the thought of it. After what he did to Alissa…there was no forgiving him for

71

that. As Japheth followed him through the building, it became clear they were going the same way. They reached a door almost simultaneously that was blocked by two large, armoured aliens.

'Name?' one of the aliens said.

Colfer was slightly ahead so answered first. 'Daniel Colfer, presence requested by Commander Garret.'

The alien motioned towards a small seating area off to the right, and Colfer frowned as he turned towards it. Japheth then introduced himself to the guards who stood aside and opened the door to the meeting room. Colfer watched open-mouthed as Japheth disappeared inside.

As he walked into the room, Japheth's eyes flickered around the table. All familiar faces. He smiled at Alissa as he approached Garret and offered his hand. She almost seemed to blush as he stepped beside her. 'It's good to see you, Garret.' The old man nodded and shook the hand that was offered. 'Thank you for coming.'

'It's my pleasure.' Japheth stepped back and glanced once more at Alissa. He winked as she made eye contact. That time she definitely blushed as she looked away.

When all were seated, the emperor looked to Garret. 'You requested our appearance. What is the purpose?'

'I want to understand how we are integrating with your people.' He paused and looked around the table. 'I'm a little behind on current affairs.'

'Two of our larger hotel installations have been donated to your people to act as homes for as long as they need. I do expect that at some point, your people will integrate with my own, so this is more of a temporary measure.'

'What about jobs? Money?' Garret asked.

'Some of your people have already found themselves positions within the community. Your doctor is working in our hospital, teaching my people how to heal humans.' He then motioned towards Japheth. 'And this gentleman has been offered a position within our street guard, to protect all the people of this city.'

Japheth smiled and looked down at the table as Alissa glanced over at him. 'I didn't know you'd taken a job?'

Japheth smiled. 'You've been avoiding me.'

The emperor watched their short exchange then continued. 'There are many areas within the city that would value the expertise offered by your people. It is my suggestion that the humans look for a place they would feel comfortable working. If there is a position available, it will be offered without hesitation.'

Garret looked over at Alissa. 'What about you, Alissa? Will our former chief of security be joining the street guard?'

Japheth's eyebrows rose as he looked over for her answer.

'Actually, Garret, I was thinking I might check in at the shipyard.' She looked down at the table as the emperor smiled.

'Marvellous! I think the shipyard would be lucky to have you on board.'

'Thank you.' Alissa smiled.

Garret's face turned stony as he spoke his next words. 'What of the Committee?'

Emperor Sorixa grimaced at the mention. 'They...cannot locate us here. Our civilisation has remained perfectly safe for many years out of the eye of the Committee.'

'But now they know we're here. If they scan the planet looking for us...'

'I'll admit, there is a risk they will search for you. But we have the capabilities to protect ourselves if necessary.' The emperor rose to his feet and grinned at the room. 'But presently, I look forward to seeing how our communities continue to combine. For now, I must depart. My work is never done.'

He chuckled as he walked out of the room, leaving the door open. The four humans remained seated for a few moments, each thinking about their own futures within the city when they heard a slight cough and a gentle knock on the open door. 'You, uh, wanted to see me, Garret?'

Colfer stood in the doorway, slightly hunched and trying not to make eye contact with those in the room. Alissa looked over and stood up. 'I've got to go.' She started making her way past Colfer when Japheth jumped to his feet and followed her.

As they left the room, Colfer stepped inside, and Alissa heard Garret's voice. 'Close the door please.' The door clicked behind them.

Japheth gently reached out for her arm as she marched down the hallway, slowing her slightly until she stopped and turned to face him. 'Are you all right?' His eyes searched her face.

'Yeah, it's just…whenever I see him, I get angry, and I know how capable I can be.' She looked down at her now clenched fists.

'Is that why you don't want to join the street guard? You're afraid of hurting someone?'

'I guess.' Alissa turned to start walking, and Japheth fell into step beside her. 'I just want to be me again. Not the killer I was turned into. I don't want to fight anymore.'

Japheth took her hand in his own, and she felt the familiar comfort of his touch.

'I'll walk you home.'

***

74

As Japeth and Alissa left City Hall, Garret sat at the table watching Colfer as he made his way around to the opposite side and sat down.

'Daniel Colfer, chief navigation officer on board The Ark.' It was a statement from Garret, not a question.

Colfer nodded. 'Yes, sir.'

'You passed the aptitude test two years ago with ninety percent accuracy.'

Colfer nodded again.

'So tell me…' Garret paused to look over Colfer who seemed very nervous. 'What happened after the ship crashed?'

'Well, sir…Alissa admitted to the people that it was all her fault. That everyone died because of her.' He swallowed hard, as if his mouth was filled with cotton wool. 'I was originally one of the people being considered for leadership, so when I heard that…I realised I had to take charge.'

Garret inhaled deeply. 'Which you did…'

'Yes, sir, I de-escalated the situation by asking the three main instigators to leave the camp.'

'Banished…I believe you used the word banished.'

Colfer paled. 'Um…yes, sir.'

Garret eased himself to his feet and took hold of his cane, slowly walking around the table to the large window. He looked out to the city below. 'How different things may have been had Alissa, Ham, and Shem not been found in time.'

'How so, sir?'

'You sentenced them to death, Colfer.' He waited for the statement to sink in. 'We may be far from Earth, but we must still maintain our honour and observe our laws.' Garret turned quickly to face Colfer, who had now broken out in a sweat. 'You decided that you would bring back the archaic practice of capital punishment. Had they died in the desert, you would be facing a long sentence in an alien prison.'

'But, sir—'

Garret raised his hand to cut him off. 'I suggest you thank whatever deity you please that they survived and then quietly live out your life here without rocking the boat. But as far as I'm concerned, you are stripped of rank and title.' He limped over to Colfer and rested a hand on his shoulder. 'I suggest you stay under the radar, Daniel.'

With that, Garret motioned to Megan and left the room.

CHAPTER NINE

THE LONG CORRIDOR TO THE APARTMENT ALISSA SHARED with Megan was very well decorated. A thick plush carpet silenced their footsteps as they walked, hand in hand towards her door. 'So, what's a sike?'

Japheth furrowed his brow. 'Where'd you hear that?'

Alissa shrugged. 'A nurse mentioned it. I overheard. Something about a handsome human man with sike skills. I figured it might be you.'

He smiled. 'A nurse says handsome and I'm the first guy you think of?'

Alissa laughed as she realised what he meant.

'No…I…well, obviously you're handsome.' Her words started to get mixed up. 'Forget I said anything, please.'

'Absolutely not.' He squeezed her hand. 'The people here believe I have psychic abilities. I had a vision of war in the streets.'

'Oh, do you think it was the future?' She looked at him as they walked. His face was a picture of concern. 'I don't know. I hope not but…after what the Committee did to me…I can't rule it out, you know?'

As they reached the door, Alissa turned to him. 'All right, so tell me what I'm thinking.'

He smiled. 'Really?'

'Sure…use your sike skills. What am I thinking right now?'

As he stared into her eyes, his brow furrowed. Alissa smirked as she let herself imagine what it would be like if he kissed her right at that moment. She felt herself flush as she looked down at his lips for a moment. He smiled and took a step closer. 'I don't have to hear your thoughts, Alissa, to know what you're thinking.'

He gently ran his hand round to the back of her neck and allowed her hair to entwine around his fingers. He leaned closer and pressed his lips to hers. Alissa kissed him back, wrapping her arms around him as he carefully pressed her against the door.

After a few moments, Japheth pulled slowly back. 'I should get going. I've got a shift in a few hours.'

'Okay.' Alissa felt a small amount of relief. Kissing him was one thing, but this could easily have moved quicker than she was ready for.

'How about I pick you up for breakfast?' He smiled.

'I'd like that.'

He leaned in and kissed her softly on the cheek before turning and walking back down the corridor. Alissa watched as he walked away.

***

Daniel Colfer was angry. He stomped through the city. Angry at the world around him, humiliated by Garret, and ready to just lash out. He marched with gritted teeth, following his path from earlier. Out past the city and into the dust. When he was far enough out that all the sounds of life had faded away, he dropped to his knees and cried out, digging his fingers into the dusty terrain beneath him. Alissa...*that bitch*...she risked the lives of every person on that ship, but she goes unpunished! She waltzes around the city like a queen and the mere mortals can only bow to her.

He punched the ground. He was going to make her pay. One way or another, she would regret the choices she made.

He rose to his feet and kicked at the sandy ground, still moving farther and farther away from the city as he ranted to himself about her. His unhealthy behaviour went on for a few hours and eventually he found himself at a guard post. He looked at the aliens and they looked back.

'Do you wish to leave the confines of the sanctuary?' they called out to him.

Colfer nodded, and they opened a small doorway out into the blazing heat.

***

Japheth couldn't help but grin as he walked through the city towards the guardhouse. He had kissed her, and she hadn't thought about Silver Glove—at least it seemed that way to him. He went into the guardhouse and walked up to the front desk. 'Japheth, I'm here for my shift.'

The portly, dark green drovian picked up a comms. 'The human is here, boss.'

A crackly voice replied, 'Send him to the third floor, room seven.'

'Boss says third floor…'

'Room seven, got it.'

79

Japheth made his way up to the required room and knocked on the door before opening it and walking in.

Behind a desk sat an older green man who motioned at an empty seat. Japheth sat down and smiled.

'Right then, there's someone coming in to work on your sike skills. Well, to test if you have them.'

'Okay...' The smile had faded from Japheth's face, and he was now worried about what he'd let himself in for.

It only took a few minutes before a woman, who couldn't have been much older than Japheth, walked down the corridor and smiled. 'You're the human siker, I presume.'

Japheth nodded and rose to his feet, offering her his hand to shake. The green woman obliged then turned to lead him back down the corridor she had appeared from.

They travelled a short distance, passing white doors along blue painted walls. Everything looked so similar in here, for a moment Japheth wondered if he would be able to find his way back out.

The woman stopped and opened one of the white doors, then she walked inside, motioning for Japheth to follow.

Inside was a metallic table and two seats. They looked remarkably uncomfortable, but Japheth was more concerned about the headpiece that hung above one of the chairs. He presumed, correctly, that he would be sitting there. He slowly moved into the room and glanced up at the wire-filled machine that dangled ominously above his head as he lowered himself onto the hard metal surface of the chair.

The woman sat opposite and smiled. 'I'm Eliana. I'm a scientist of sorts. My speciality is sikers.'

Japheth nodded along as she spoke.

'I'm here to make a diagnosis. Not all people who have a vision are gifted. Most are just in the right place at the right time.'

Japheth furrowed his brow. 'I don't follow…'

She smiled again. 'On this world, psychic energy is constantly flowing. Mostly it's imperceptible, but sometimes a wave is strong enough to be seen if someone stands in its peak. Seeing a vision in this way doesn't make you a siker.'

'So, I could just have been standing in the peak of a psychic wave?'

She nodded. 'Very much so. It does happen from time to time.' She motioned upwards. 'The device above your head will measure the imprint of the wave you experienced and establish its strength. If it is below the threshold, then it's very likely that you are a siker.'

'Is it painful?'

Eliana shook her head. 'Absolutely not. Your mind will replay the vision you saw. You won't be aware of your current surroundings. It will feel, for you, as though you are standing and experiencing the vision firsthand.'

'All right.' Japheth nodded. and Eliana stood and moved swiftly round the table.

Taking the headpiece in both hands, she gently lowered it onto Japheth's head. 'All right, I'm going to activate the device. Prepare yourself.'

Taking a deep breath, Japheth closed his eyes and clasped his hands in his lap. The next few seconds felt like an eternity, until suddenly, he was back on the street. Hundreds of small ships darted about the skies, shooting down civilians. He watched again as the Drovians fell to the attack. In the distance, he saw a woman running through the streets. He watched as she ran towards a Drovian child who was cowering behind an upturned car. Last time the vision had faded so fast, but now, it felt as though he could explore. He ran towards her as one of the ships came low, shooting along the ground towards her. Japheth stood, frozen in horror as the

81

woman used her own body to protect the child. He cried out in anguish as the vision faded and he was back in the room.

Sweat poured from his forehead, and his fists were clenched so tightly his nails had made little half-moon slits in his flesh.

'What the hell…' was all he managed to say in between breaths.

'It seems as though you weren't *riding the wave*, as they say.' Eliana lifted the headpiece gently upwards, relieving some of the pressure on Japheth's skull. 'You are a true siker.'

'What does that mean?' He looked up at the green woman.

'It means you are a valuable asset.' She turned and walked back to her seat. 'We would like to help you explore your abilities.'

Japheth sat back in the chair; his head was throbbing. 'How exactly?'

Eliana smiled. 'A lot of it is natural ability. You'll be partnered with a law keeper and patrol the streets. You should receive visions as you work.'

Japheth nodded once more. 'Okay, when do we start?'

***

Alissa circled the vehicle that was hovering in the open space and frowned. The man following her was the yardmaster. He would decide if she had the skills to work in the shop. It was a busy place with the constant drone of engines as cars and ships were circled through the repair process. The yardmaster had committed himself to allowing humans to work with them, but only the best would get in.

Alissa felt the same nerves as the day she sat down to take the aptitude test. She shook her head and scolded herself internally. This was her forte, her chosen career, and she intended to wow them all.

After dropping to her knees, Alissa leaned under the small car, although, it did look more like a ship. There was a dark stain on the ground beneath it. She gently traced her fingers along the pipework and found a small puncture in a rubber tube. She rubbed it between her fingers, feeling the texture, then brought it to her nose to smell the fluid. 'Oil.' She turned to the yardmaster. 'There's a leak. They're losing lubricant so the engine is seizing.'

The yardmaster nodded. 'And what is the solution?'

'Simple—replace the pipe and the fluid then check the engine for burned out parts.' Alissa smiled. This felt right.

***

The gates of the Through and Through stood tall and open, welcoming travellers and preparing them for the journey. It was a rail system that travelled directly through the core of the planet to a second underground city on the other side.

It was already quite busy—people in suits waiting for a ride to work, families going on a day out, even humans wanting to explore.

Shem manoeuvred his way through the crowd and looked for the manager's office. One of the Drovians told him they were always looking for transport pilots, and he was ready to take a job. Working would be a welcome distraction from thinking about Alissa.

Once he reached the door, he pressed the panel to alert someone to his presence. After a few moments, the door slid open and a short, slightly fat, and very bald Drovian man stood there.

'What can I do for you?' His voice was crackly and high.

Shem smiled down at him. 'I'm looking for work.'

The Drovian looked Shem up and down. 'What is it you do?'

'Well,' Shem started, 'I was a navigation officer in a former life. I'd make a pretty decent pilot.'

The Drovian slowly nodded. 'All right…follow me.'

He led Shem through the crowd and to the front of the platform, which was a huge ring with a hole in the centre. 'You ever seen a T and T before?'

Shem shook his head. 'Not exactly, but it sounds similar to the subway systems we had back home.'

'So…the carriage will arrive shortly. It'll come up through the hole. The customers'—he motioned to the people on the platform—'they'll board and strap in. Then the pilot on the underside will control the descent.'

Shem nodded along. 'I guess then once you reach the halfway point there's a pilot on the other side to finish the journey.'

The Drovian smiled. 'Yes…yes. You're a quick study.' The man edged closer to the hole. 'Now, we will head down into the lower pilot deck and they'll give you the tour. If you're still interested in piloting this thing once you've had a taste, then we will get you all signed up.'

'Thank you, sir.' Shem smiled. 'I think this is gonna be really good.'

Within minutes, the platform started to vibrate and the shuttle slowly emerged, raising up until the doors that circled its shell were above ground. The Drovian man pressed a button next to the door closest them, and it slid open with a hiss. Shem walked inside and looked around. The shuttle was massive with hanging rails that were quickly being grabbed by green hands.

'Everyone stands in here?'

The Drovian nodded. 'Of course.'

'Isn't that dangerous?'

'The shuttle is fitted with inertial dampeners. No matter how fast we go, you can't even tell you're moving.'

The inside of the shuttle was doughnut-shaped, and there was a wall surrounding the hole in the centre. The Drovian opened a slender panel and disappeared inside. Once through, Shem saw a ladder—you could go either way. As they stood watching, a panel opened above them and large boot-clad feet appeared. Climbing down past them was the current driver.

'Come on, Shem. We're following him down.'

CHAPTER TEN

THE HARSH SUN BURNED INTO COLFER'S FLESH. THIS truly was a desert. But out here, at least, no one hated him. That was the reality for the former navigation chief. He was nothing but the heartless man who had tried to kill three members of the crew.

He took a mouthful of the cool water he had brought with him and bitterly trudged towards the crash site. The thought was, he would find a way to live out here. He would prove that it wasn't a death sentence and that Alissa and her friends just weren't capable of survival, and that really wasn't his fault.

Then they would have to forgive him.

It took him a while, but Colfer eventually reached the first remnants of the shattered ship he had once called home. It was still just as devastating as the day they had crashed. There were still bodies out here, buried under mounds of twisted steel. Thousands of people they would never find. He felt a lump hardening in his throat and swallowed it down.

This was all Alissa's fault.

He found a metal cabinet that had a rainbow hue from where it had burned in the crash and the doors were twisted just enough that they wouldn't fully close. But it was enough. Colfer gently placed some Drovian ration packs inside and sat on the dusty ground under the blazing sun.

As he drew patterns in the sand, he saw a figure approaching in the distance, nothing more than a silhouette against the bright sky. As they got closer, he could see it was a woman. A Drovian with pale green skin and the bluest eyes he'd ever seen.

As she got closer, she held out her hand. 'A traditional Earth greeting, I believe.'

Colfer jumped to his feet and reached his own hand out to meet hers. 'Yeah…it is.' He furrowed his brow. 'What are you doing all the way out here?'

The woman smiled. 'I need your help. My people are in grave danger.'

Colfer looked down at his feet. 'Because my people have invaded.'

'No…you're welcome in our home. But…humans bring danger with them.'

'The Committee.'

'Yes. My people will be destroyed.'

Colfer shifted uncomfortably. 'What do you want me to do?'

The Drovian woman held out her hand. In it was a small metal sphere.

'Take this back to the city and hide it somewhere.'

Colfer reached out and took the sphere. It was lighter than he expected and very cold to the touch. He rolled it between his hands. 'What is it?'

'An alarm system. If the Committee manage to get into the city, it will warn us.'

Colfer frowned again. 'Why can't you take it in?'

'Because I don't live in the city anymore. I was banished.'

'Why?'

A sad smile crossed her face. 'I made some bad choices. There's a place out here for people like us. The ones that don't belong in the city.'

'Really?'

She nodded. 'When you've completed your task, you are welcome to join us, Colfer.'

***

Alissa skipped into the shipyard for her first shift as an engineer. It had been a long time coming, but she finally felt like her life was slipping into a state of normality.

Living with Megan had been tough at first, and learning each other's routines was no easy task. Megan was a bit of a neat freak by Alissa's standards, and the doctor considered the former assassin to be cluttered and chaotic.

Japheth was becoming a regular visitor as well. He could come and take Alissa out for walks through the city or out for meals. He told her what it was like working with the guard force, protecting the citizens. And Alissa would listen with wide eyes and a smile.

As she crossed the open yard, her boss called out to her, 'Hey, human girl. Bay seventeen is yours today.'

She eyed up the area and saw a royal-blue car sitting heavily on the concrete. It was definitely supposed to be floating.

'Sure thing, boss,' Alissa called back as she dumped her jacket in her locker and grabbed her tool belt. Walking back over to the car, she began to think out loud. 'Okay, car. What's wrong with you?' Alissa mumbled to herself as she crouched down, opened the side panel, and started checking the plasma flow tubes.

'All right, no visible cracks. Let's see what happens when we turn you on.'

She stood and turned towards the front of the car to get to the ignition. As she turned, she saw a man standing at the back of the bay, staring at her with his piercing blue eyes. Then everything faded to black.

'Alissa?' The voice was comforting, familiar. 'Are you all right?'

Alissa sat up and rubbed the sore lump on the back of her head as she opened her eyes. She was on the cold floor, and Ham was crouched in front of her. 'You really took a tumble, Al. What happened?'

Visions of the man with the piercing blue eyes danced in her mind. 'Something's wrong, Ham.'

CHAPTER ELEVEN

'WHAT EXACTLY DID YOU SEE?'

Alissa looked around the room as Garret spoke. As soon as she told Ham about Blue Eyes, he had panicked and dragged her straight to Megan, who in turn had called the meeting. They had all learned that when Alissa saw something, they should pay attention.

She looked over to Japheth, who was watching her closely with his brow furrowed.

'Well, I turned around and he was just…there. Staring at me.'

Megan shook her head. 'I don't understand. You destroyed their ship. This blue eyed man should be dead. They shouldn't be able to get in your head.'

'Maybe you missed something,' Shem mumbled, staring at his hands. He had avoided making eye contact with Alissa since he had arrived.

'Holo projector?'

The room turned to look at Ham. 'I mean, they've done it before.'

The emperor shook his head. 'No, no, no. They don't know where the city is. They wouldn't be able to get one in here.'

'Well then, I'm going crazy.' Alissa buried her face in her hands. 'I don't want to see him.'

'Who?' Japheth asked softly.

'Silver Glove.' Shem's voice was bitter as he spoke for the first time. 'If they're using Blue Eyes, then it's only a matter of time before they pull out the big gun.'

'He's right.' Alissa's voice was muffled by her hands.

'So what do we do?' Japheth was on his feet. 'We need answers dammit.'

'If the Committee is indeed in the city, then we have a grave problem.' The emperor stood slowly. 'We will scan the city for alien technology. Something that is neither Drovian nor human.'

'And I'll check Alissa over. Your hospital facilities are more advanced than what I had on The Ark. If there's alien tech inside Alissa's head, I'll find it.' Megan's voice was determined and yet still kind enough to rouse Alissa from hiding behind her hands, she was quiet as she asked. 'When do we start?'

'I'll need a couple of hours to prep.' Megan looked at her hands.

Alissa nodded. 'All right. I think I'm gonna take a walk.'

With that, she stood up and left the room. Glances were exchanged by the remaining occupants of the table.

'I'm gonna go with her.' Japheth turned to walk towards the door as Shem rose to his feet.

'No.'

The entire room turned to look at him.

'I'm going,' Shem said.

He pushed past Japheth and left to follow Alissa.

When he finally caught up to her, she was already halfway down the street.

'Hey, wait up!'

Alissa stopped at the sound of his voice. It was the last person she expected to follow her. They hadn't spoken in weeks. When he caught up to her, she started walking once more as Shem fell into step beside her.

The silence between them was painful. Alissa wanted nothing more than to bare her soul to her best friend. But she couldn't.

'What's on your mind, Al?'

'Nothing.' Alissa stared at the floor as they walked.

'Liar.'

She could hear the smile in his voice, and it irritated her enough that she stopped in the middle of the path and turned to Shem. 'What are you doing?'

'What?' Shem looked confused.

'You follow me out here and try the whole laughing-and-joking thing. Acting like everything is okay between us.'

'Al...I...'

Shem tried to get words out, but Alissa had no intention of listening. '*You kicked me out!*' Tears of frustration threatened to fall, but still she continued, 'You were supposed to be my best friend, Shem. But you hurt me.' Her tears now fell freely. 'Do you hear me, Shem Mitchell? You. Hurt. Me!'

'I know.' Shem's head was hanging low. 'I messed up.'

Alissa watched as he took a deep breath and then looked up, his eyes meeting hers.

'I'm so sorry, Alissa. I let jealousy ruin us. But I get it now—you don't love me in the way I wanted, and as much as that sucks for me, I don't want to live my life without you in it.' Shem reached out and took Alissa's hand. 'If you love Japheth, then that's none of my business and I'll support you. I just want to be your friend again.'

One solitary tear slid down his cheek, and Alissa reached up to wipe it away.

'You're such an idiot.' She smiled and wrapped him in a hug. 'I missed you, Shem.'

He held her tightly. 'Right back at you.'

***

Colfer sat on a piece of metal under the hot sun. He had planted the sphere and now he would be taken back to the camp for banished Drovians. He would finally have a place to call home. One where he wasn't thought of as the man who tried to kill The Ark's sweetheart, *Alissa Namaah.*

He grunted as he thought of her. Little Miss Perfect, the woman who was responsible for the deaths of thousands of innocent people. People who burned as their ship crashed to the surface. It was her fault, and yet they all still loved her. He slammed his fist into the metal cabinet he was sitting on, splitting the skin on his knuckle. He watched as drops of ruby pattered into the newly made dent, until something caught his eye.

He squinted into the distance to see a handful of figures heading his way. It was hard to make out, but none of them looked like the woman he had met. In fact, it looked almost as though they had multiple legs. He rubbed his palms into his eyes and looked again, this time trying to shield his eyes from the glare of the sun with his hand. They weren't humanoid. Their bodies were too low to the ground and their legs stuck out at unnatural angles. As they closed in, he could see their heads were too big and a strange shape as well, triangular, almost like an ant.

That's when it hit him—they were insectoid. Like nothing he had ever seen. He felt his blood run cold, and with all the effort he could muster, Colfer ran.

He didn't get far before he felt the sting of a plasma shot hit him in the back. His legs fell from under him, and he lay, facedown in the sand. He tried to stand, but his legs wouldn't respond. In desperation, he resorted to dragging himself along the desert on his belly.

He could hear them clicking. It was the worst sound he had ever heard. Completely inhuman. They were close. Panic rose like bile in his throat, and he started crying out to anyone that could hear, 'Please…someone…help me…'

He felt another sting, and suddenly it felt as though his entire body had exploded in pain. Fire ripped through his veins as he desperately tried to escape. The last thing he saw before the world went black was the long slender feet of one of the creatures as it loomed over him.

CHAPTER TWELVE

JAPHETH WALKED INTO THE GUARDHOUSE, HIS MIND   running through the day's events. How had one of the aliens found them here? It was supposed to be a secret. They were supposed to be safe. He turned the corner towards the office he had been given and opened the door. It was a small room with a polystyrene-type substance coating the walls, which had also been painted an unfortunate shade of beige. There were two desks—one was his and one belonged to his partner Garyx.

Japheth crossed the small room and sat down at his desk, staring at the wall. He felt powerless to help, and with each passing moment, his frustration grew. Alissa was going to blame Silver Glove for this. And it would make it all the more difficult for her to see Japheth for who he was. He despised the fact that he shared a face with the man who had traumatised Alissa. He would do anything to fix this, to help her.

While he wallowed in self-pity, the door opened again revealing Garyx. His skin was a deep forest green and his hardened eyes were almost black. He wore a long brown trench coat and a gun strapped to his hip. 'Hey, you ready to get out there?'

Japheth looked up at his partner. 'What?'

Garyx sniffed. 'Announcement from the emperor. There's potentially a threat in the city. He wants sikes out on the street.'

'Right…sure.' Japheth stood and headed to the door.

Garyx grabbed his arm gently. 'You all right?'

Japheth nodded slightly. 'Yeah…let's go.'

The two men made their way down to the street and began their foot patrol. Garyx walked slowly. He said it was so that he could attune to the energies of the city, so that if there was a threat, he would sense the vision and get to the right place.

Japheth found it to be a difficult concept to follow but tried his best to clear his mind and step slowly beside his partner.

'You already knew about the threat, didn't you?' Garyx asked in his gravelly voice.

'Yeah.'

'And it's not because you had a vision.'

'No.'

Garyx nodded to himself and continued in silence for a few more minutes. 'It's that girl of yours, ain't it?'

'She's not mine.'

'You sure about that?' Garyx was looking at Japheth as they walked. 'You sure spend a lot of time thinking about her.'

Japheth stopped open-mouthed and glared at Garyx who carried on with his slow walk.

98

'Get out of my head, Garyx.' Japheth practically growled the words, which made his partner stop and very slowly turn to look at him.

'I'm not in your head. You're practically screaming from the top of your psychic lungs.'

'What?'

'Being near you, Japheth, as a sike, it's difficult. You project a constant desire for this woman.'

Japheth's shoulders slumped. 'I got it bad, huh?'

Garyx smiled and put his hand gently on Japheth's shoulder. 'Yeah, but that ain't so wrong, you know.'

As the two men started their slow walk, once more Japheth felt a pull in the back of his mind. Something was here, close by. It felt both familiar and frightening. He stopped and closed his eyes, trying to focus on the feeling. He could hear Garyx talking, but he sounded far away, mumbling something about finding the wave.

In the darkness of his mind's eye, Japheth saw someone walking towards him. A man in a suit. A man with a silver hand.

***

'So, how has life been at Megan's?' Shem handed Alissa a cold drink from the vendor in the park then sat beside her on the bench.

'It's been nice. She's a bit of a neat freak but, it's nice.' Alissa focussed hard on the drink in her hand as she talked.

99

'It's just been weird, you know? Living in an underground alien city. It doesn't seem quite real.'

Shem nodded. 'I know what you mean. I've been working the T&T and something about flying a shuttle through the centre of the planet feels insane.'

'What if he's really here, Shem?'

'Who?'

'The blue-eyed guy.' Alissa shifted uncomfortably as she spoke. 'What if they've found us? Then it's just a matter of time before they wipe us out.'

'Well, Al, I've got no plans to die today. So I guess if they are here, they're gonna have a real fight on their hands.'

Alissa smiled at Shem. 'When did you get so brave?'

'Probably when I punched Ryan in the face.' Shem smiled sadly. 'You know I found him, in the wreckage.' Shem sighed heavily. 'He died, and yet here we are, walking around like everything's normal.'

'You've got to let that guilt go, Shem. Or it's gonna eat you alive.'

'I really messed up, Alissa. I keep thinking back to the old days, in New Amerland.' He paused, looking down at the drink in his hand. 'I passed the test without even studying. Did I tell you that?'

Alissa shook her head.

'It comes naturally to me, numbers and equations. All that time wasted, I should have been helping you.'

'What?'

'I knew even then that you hated studying and you hated tests even more. If I'd helped you, you would have passed.'

Alissa smiled and took his hand. 'You don't know that, Shem.'

'Yeah, I do! And if you'd passed, you would have had your ticket and you'd still be…' Shem paused.

'I'd still be yours? That clumsy girl that had no friends except you and Ham.'

Shem looked down while Alissa carried on. 'Shem, I don't regret who I've become. Not anymore. In fact, I'm kind of proud. It's not all roses, but it's not the Hell I thought it would be.'

Shem stood up. 'Come on. We'd better get you to Megan.'

***

The first sensation Colfer could feel was the cold, smooth floor beneath his face. It was a stark contrast to the sand that was under him. He remembered falling and the pain. They had shot him! The insect creatures.

With a groan, Colfer rolled himself onto his back and opened his eyes. His clothes felt stiff and his shirt stuck to the skin on his back. Looking down, he let out a groan. His clothes were soaked in blood he assumed was his own, and the moment he rolled onto his back he screamed. The dull pain he felt in his back exploded in agony as it took his full weight.

In a panic, he flipped back over and pulled himself up onto his hands and knees. He wiped the tears of pain that were blurring his eyes and took in his surroundings. Dark metallic walls that matched the floor in size and design made the room feel so tiny. This was a cube with nothing but a door in one wall.

With a slight whimper, Colfer pushed against the door. It was locked. *Obviously,* he thought. He banged his fist a couple of times. 'Hey! Let me out of here!'

Bang bang bang.

'I helped you! I'm on your side!'

Bang bang bang.

'Please…I think I need a doctor…'

Colfer slid to the floor, still holding a fist against the door. His voice was nothing more than a whisper now. 'What have I done?'

He sat there for hours, on the cold hard floor. He could feel the gentle trickle of warm sticky blood from the open wound on his back. Eventually the door slid gently aside and Colfer crumpled onto the floor in the hallway. Looking up weakly, he saw the insectoid faces looking back down at him, guns in hand.

'Get up.'

Colfer tried to push himself away from the floor, but his arms buckled under him.

'I said get up!' The barrel of one of the guns pressed painfully into the side of his head. 'Or I'll paint the deck with your brains, human.'

'I can't…please…' No more words came out as Colfer slipped once more into darkness.

***

'Listen, I was thinking, after the brain scans maybe I could take you out. For some food and a drink? There's some great places, Al. I think you'll really like them.'

Alissa glanced over at Shem while he spoke. It was clear he was trying very hard not to look at her while he asked. Alissa took his hand and stopped him from walking. 'That sounds like it would be fun. We should invite Ham as well.'

Shem looked at his feet and nodded slightly. 'Yeah, you're right.' He looked back up to meet Alissa' gaze. 'The three of us, back together at last.'

He smiled what felt to Alissa like the most genuine smile she had seen from him in a long time.

'Hey, there's this one place that literally just puts huge trays of food on tables and you just take whatever you want.'

Alissa raised her eyebrows. 'Seriously?'

Shem nodded enthusiastically. 'Yeah, and not a cabbage risotto in sight.'

He laughed while Alissa stared at him for a second before joining in.

'Hey, do you ever miss Saime's?'

Shem turned to look at her while they walked. 'You mean the greasy glasses, dirty tables, and booze that tasted like battery acid?'

Alissa nodded. 'Yeah…'

Shem paused for a second before he spoke. 'I was in a bar three nights ago. This sweet woman comes up and shows me to my seat, hands me a menu, and tells me humans drink free for one hour.'

Alissa laughed. 'What! That's insane!'

'Right! That's what I thought!'

Alissa caught a look of sadness as it crossed Shem's face. 'The glass was clean, and the drink tasted like the nectar of the Gods.' He laughed. 'Seriously, it was amazing. But I couldn't help but think about those greasy glasses, dirty tables, and booze that tasted like battery acid.'

Alissa put her hand on his arm as he continued. 'It's not that I miss Saime's particularly. Or even New Amerland for that matter.' He sighed heavily. 'I just miss the way life used to be. When the most dramatic decision we had to make was whether we should eat a boiled potato or toast with our fake bacon.'

Alissa laughed bitterly. 'I miss it too, sometimes. But look how far we've come.' She motioned to the city surrounding them. 'We are literally living on an alien world.'

They turned the corner as they spoke, and Alissa's heart felt like it stopped beating. She could feel Shem's hand intertwine with her own and grip tightly. Her whole body turned cold as she looked right at the man with the Silver Glove. He turned to her, and his lips twisted into a sinister smile. 'Did you miss me, my love?'

CHAPTER THIRTEEN

HE FELT THE SEARING PAIN BEFORE HE WAS FULLY   conscious. Colfer unwillingly opened his eyes and took in his new surroundings. Gone was the cube he had previously resided in, and instead he was strapped to a metal table that was, unfortunately for him, almost completely vertical. But with his arms and legs pinned down by metal shackles, he had little chance of collapsing again.

His vision blurred dangerously as he looked around. This place looked like a medical unit, sterile and cold with a table of ominous tools beside him. He tried to speak, but his tongue rolled heavily around in his open mouth.

On the other side of the room, two men stood over a counter with their backs to him. The tinny clang of metal on metal rang through the small room as Colfer struggled weakly against his bonds. 'Please, let me go.'

One of the men turned and shook his head slowly in Colfer's direction before once again turning to face the counter. Through the blur, all he could make out was that the men weren't human, or any other race he'd seen so far. They were blue-skinned, but he couldn't see their features. 'Please, I've done nothing wrong. I helped you!'

They didn't even turn this time, but a cold voice echoed through the chamber, emanating from behind Colfer.

'Yes…you did.'

He heard footsteps, and a man came into view. His skin was a deep blue, but still blurred.

'You helped us locate their city. And as we speak, a team are on their way to destroy the emperor.'

Colfer blinked hard. 'Why?'

'Because the Drovians were supposed to be dead, and I can't have anyone finding out they survived our onslaught.'

Colfer shook his head. 'No…I don't understand. Who are you?'

'You may address me as Xyan. I am the commanding officer of Project Black.'

'What's that?'

Xyan smiled as the other two men in the room brought him a tray of silver tools. He gently picked one up.

'Now…this device will allow me to pinpoint a nerve within your skin and slowly peel it free from your flesh.'

Colfer fought once more against his bonds. 'No…please…'

'Have you found yourself more willing to share information with me?'

'Yes…anything…'

106

Xyan leaned in close, his pronounced brow becoming clearer as he came into focus. He said slowly and deliberately, 'Where is Alissa?'

Colfer furrowed his brow. 'Why do you want her?'

The alien man leaned in close. 'She murdered my wife. The general on board the Ik'Omeg.'

'I knew I was right about her.' Colfer's aching face changed into a look of set determination. 'How do I help?'

***

'You can't be here.' Alissa voice shook as she spoke. 'You're dead.'

Silver Glove laughed gently and stepped closer. 'Oh, darling, not even death could keep me from you.'

Shem stepped in front of Alissa. 'How are you doing this?'

'The knowledge of the hologram was uploaded. I know everything he knew. I feel everything he felt.'

Alissa shuddered. 'No.'

'Yes, Alissa.' He stepped closer still. 'I know what it felt like to hold your hand in the facility, to kiss you…and to kill you.'

'I'm warning you…' Shem spoke through gritted teeth as Silver Glove laughed but never took his eyes off Alissa.

'My pet, you and I have been more intimate in your dreams than any man in your waking life. You belong to me.'

Shem took a swing at Silver Glove, who dodged the attack and pushed him aside easily, barely breaking stride as he closed the gap between himself and Alissa.

'You can't fight this, love.'

Alissa stood perfectly still, watching as her tormentor grew ever nearer.

'It's wonderful to see I still have such power over you.'

And suddenly he was standing right in front of her, smiling, leaning in.

With a balled fist, Alissa connected with his cheekbone, sending him staggering.

'You have no power over me anymore.'

Japheth and Garyx turned the corner just in time to see Alissa punch Silver Glove.

'She's got one hell of a right hook.' Garyx looked impressed as Japheth set off at a run, connecting with Silver Glove and sending them both tumbling to the ground.

Alisa jumped into action, pulling Japheth onto his feet and away from Silver Glove, then standing between the two of them. She glared at Silver Glove. 'Whatever you're planning…it's not gonna work.'

He smiled his sickeningly handsome smile. 'But, my darling…it already has.'

With that, he faded into blue light and was gone.

***

Garret sat in the boardroom in the heart of the City Hall. Once Alissa had finished with her scans she would join Garret and the emperor to discuss options. He flicked his finger over a comms pad, reading the local news for the city, scouring to see if there were any clues to explain the sudden appearance of the alien threat, and coming up empty.

His knees ached as he waited. This quiet retirement wasn't quite what he had expected. He rubbed his temples as his mind wandered. He thought about the first time he had met Alissa, how young she had seemed and so broken.

But now, she had grown into herself. Her time on the Ark had proven that, and he was proud to say she had done it under his command.

As he sat reminiscing, the door to the meeting room slid open and a group of four Drovians entered. Garret looked over, confused as to their presence. 'This building should've been cleared for the emperor's arrival.' He paused and rose to his feet slowly. 'What is your purpose here?'

The tallest of the four stepped forward. 'We have been invited to attend the meeting.'

'By whom?' Garret's voice was firm.

'The emperor himself. He required us to discuss…recent security issues.' The man stepped closer to Garret. 'You may leave.'

One of the Drovians shifted uncomfortably at the back, fiddling with something in his hand. Garret looked from him to the Drovian at the front.

'I will do no such thing.' Garret took hold of his cane and rested on it. 'This involves my crew.' He felt safer having a makeshift weapon in the form of his walking stick but still felt uneasy.

The Drovian rolled his eyes. 'Garret, I suggest you leave now.'

'How do you know who I am?'

'I make it my business to know the names of all the residents and crew of the Ark.'

Garret frowned. 'For what purpose? Almost all of them died in the crash.'

The Drovian's eye twitched. 'Fine…remain if you please. It will make no difference to the outcome.'

Garret looked again at the twitchy Drovian in the back. 'And what do you expect the outcome to be?' His eyes flickered back to the alien he was speaking to.

'What?'

'If you're supposed to be here, you must know what we will be discussing. So I'll ask you again, what do you expect the outcome to be?'

The Drovian looked away, thinking about an answer when the one at the back flashed a little more of the device than expected. Garret saw a short metal shaft, small lights, and the thing that for many years gave him nightmares. A big red button.

He had seen enough of them in his time in the fleet to know exactly what the creature was holding, and his blood ran cold.

While he stared, he heard the Drovian continuing their conversation. 'I expect the emperor will make the right decision.'

Garret looked back to the Drovian. 'I'm sure he will.' As soon as the words left his lips, Garret whipped his cane and brought it to meet the face of the alien standing before him. He

110

dropped it with the force of the impact, and then he grunted through the pain of his knees cracking as he leapt forward at the Drovian imposter holding the device.

He tackled him into the door and reached for his hands. The two of them were locked in a fight for control.

'Garret…' The man he hit was standing above him, looking down at his prey with a gun in hand. 'Let go of the detonator or I'll shoot.'

Garret looked up at him. 'What was the plan? Not suicide, so you plant this in the room somewhere. To go off when you leave?'

'You're smart for an old man. Now let go slowly or I'll kill you.'

Garret looked down at the device, half in his hands and half in the hands of an alien. 'You'll kill me anyway.' He sighed and moved his hand slightly. 'So I'll take us all instead.'

With that, his hand clamped firmly down onto the red button, and the world went white.

CHAPTER FOURTEEN

AS SILVER GLOVE LAUGHED, THEY HEARD AN almighty explosion. Alarms began blaring from the direction of City Hall, and Alissa felt her heart sink. 'Garret's in there.'

She set off at a run, Silver Glove's laughter still echoing in her ears as she sped away, round the corner and down a few blocks. The air got dustier as she ran. The closer she got to City Hall, the more difficult it became to keep up her speed.

There was nothing left of City Hall but lower walls and foundations. Drovians stood on the square looking over the destruction, holding each other. Alissa ran past them trying to get to the building but was quickly detained by the guards. 'I'm sorry, but you can't go any farther.'

Alissa struggled. 'But my friend! He was in there!'

The guards didn't loosen their grip on her arms. 'The building was cleared. There was only one human casualty.'

'Who?' Alissa demanded. 'Who was it?'

'The former captain of your ship, I believe.'

Alissa immediately felt weak. Her struggle eased, and if the guards hadn't been holding her, she would've sank to the floor. They gently eased her down and moved to keep the Drovian civilians from approaching the site of the explosion.

Alissa lay on the ground, sobbing openly as Shem and Japheth arrived at her side.

'Alissa, come on. We gotta go,' Shem spoke gently as he crouched by her side.

'No, Shem. It's over. We'll never escape them.' Fresh tears fell through racked sobs.

Shem looked to Japheth. 'What do we do?'

Japheth knelt down at Alissa's side and held her hand. 'If we don't fight now, then Garret's death was pointless. And that'll be on you.'

Alissa looked at him. 'How can you say that?'

'Because it's true. This city needs you to get up and go to war to protect its people.'

Alissa sniffled. 'I can't.'

'Yes, you can!' Japheth gripped her hand tighter. 'No one has ever been more capable than you. Now get up.'

Japheth rose to his feet and pulled Alissa up as well.

As Alissa pulled herself together, Garyx approached the group. 'I hate to interrupt, but the emperor wants to see you.'

'Where is he?' Shem looked at Garyx.

'He's with the minor elected officials. He was updating them before going to City Hall.'

They made their way through the city. Alissa wordlessly followed the others as they talked theories.

'It was obviously the Committee.' Shem's voice was strained as he spoke.

Japheth kept his low. 'I'd be careful saying that out loud. You'll start a mass panic.'

'A war will start a panic!' Shem was losing his composure and Japheth didn't speak again.

They reached the office block. The emperor was stood outside, waiting for them. He looked tired but as the humans got closer he took Alissa by the hand and pulled her closer. 'I'm so sorry about Garret. He was a good man.'

Alissa just nodded while she looked at her feet.

Japheth looked at the emperor. 'What do we do now?'

***

Colfer sat in a metal chair facing three aliens. The one in the centre, who had identified himself as this ship's general, stood, looming over Colfer and grinning.

'Tell me, where in the city does Alissa reside?'

Colfer shifted slightly in his chair. 'What are you doing to do to her?'

Xyan smiled in a cruel way, and Colfer felt himself shrink down in the chair. 'I'm going to hurt her. I want her to feel the torment she put me through, and by the time I've finished with her, she will beg for death.'

'But if she committed a crime, surely she should be on trial?' Colfer asked.

'Oh no, human. This is personal. Now tell me, where does she reside?'

Glancing around the room, Colfer quickly realised he was stuck in a bad situation. 'I…I don't actually know. It's not like we were friends.'

'Still, I think you do know.' The general shifted closer. 'Now tell me.'

Colfer shook his head. 'I can't…I won't.'

A low growl came from Xyan as he lifted the side of the chair with one arm and flung it at Colfer across the room. He hit the wall hard and felt blood dripping down his face. 'I have been reasonable with you, human, but you are testing the limits of my patience.' He crossed the room and took hold of Colfer's shirt, lifting him off the ground. 'I would not recommend lying again.'

Feeling dizzy and scared, Colfer looked at the crazed creature holding him up in the air. He struggled to breathe but forced his words out carefully.

'I…won't…tell…you…anything.'

Suddenly he felt the floor as he landed hard and the general crossed the room back to his companions. 'Put him back in the cell. He will break eventually.'

***

'Come in! We need to figure out what's going on.'

The emperor ushered Shem, Japheth, and the silent Alissa into the building. They followed taupe corridors until they reached a small office. It was sparsely decorated, just a desk and a chair.

'I want to make sure no one hears us.' The emperor hung his head. 'I unfortunately don't know who to trust.'

'What do you mean?' Japheth leaned against the desk.

'Well, a piece of technology was found, a projector of sorts. There are files on them in the archives, but no one has seen one since the original Committee attack. But we think they're—'

'Holograms,' Alissa said, cutting him off. 'The men I saw were holograms.'

The emperor nodded. 'Yes…however, the people who carried out the attack on City Hall were real enough, but they used holo tech to mask their appearance. Essentially, they can be anyone. Move unnoticed.'

'Then how do you know to trust us?' Alissa looked at him for the first time and saw concern in his face.

He gently rested a hand on her shoulder. 'The Committee wouldn't cry over the death of a human as you do.'

'But why? Why did they attack?' Shem chipped in for the first time since they arrived at the office. 'City Hall was cleared out for us. What was the point of blowing it up?'

Japheth sniffed hard. 'Maybe it was an accident. Maybe they were waiting for you, Emperor.'

'If they were waiting, then it wasn't an accident. It was Garret.' Alissa's voice was quiet but calm. 'He would've done this to save us.'

'Then what's the next step?'

The emperor walked towards the door. 'I have to activate the city's defences. I'm the only one that can.'

'That explains why they wanted to kill you before the fight starts.' Shem shook his head in disbelief. 'How did they even find the city? I thought you said we were hidden from them!'

'As unpleasant an accusation as it may be, I must say, I believe a human has led them to us.'

Alissa shook her head. 'I think I know which one.'

The small group was escorted in an armoured vehicle to the defence HQ on the outskirts of the city. The emperor commanded the guards to wait and took only the humans with him.

They entered the facility and walked the large metal corridors for what felt like ages. It reminded Alissa of New Amerland. She almost felt like if she turned a corner, Saime's would be there, grumpy bartender waiting inside with a dirty drink for her.

The place was massive, and they followed the emperor to the very heart of the complex structure.

'All right, I'll enter the keycodes and the defences will arm. Full shield barriers and automated weaponry will destroy anyone trying to enter the city.' With his shoulders slumped and his quiet voice, the emperor looked heartbroken.

Alissa watched as he gently and expertly navigated the system, entering code after code to get through the firewalls.

Shem leaned closer to her as she watched. 'You think Colfer did this?'

Alissa glanced in Shem's direction. 'Can you think of anyone else who hates us like he does?'

117

Shem shook his head. 'I just can't believe he would betray us.'

'Well, he thinks we did it to him first.'

Shem's brow furrowed as Alissa continued. 'All he knows is I risked the whole ship for one man.' She glanced at Japheth then back to Shem. 'All those people died in the crash because of us. He lost people too, Shem.'

'It doesn't justify selling us out to the enemy.'

'I know, but he wants revenge. I don't think you'll ever truly understand what it's like to hate someone so much you would destroy their whole world just to ruin them.'

Shem shook his head. 'And you do?'

'Are you really asking me that?'

Looking down at his hands, Shem sighed heavily. 'I guess not.'

Before Alissa could speak again, Japheth's hand slammed onto the console nearest to them while his other hand gripped his head. He cried out in pain and dropped to his knees as Alissa and Shem ran to his side. 'Japheth, what is it? What's happening?' Alissa's voice came out confident but inside she was terrified. What if they'd done someone to Japheth? Was she about to lose him here?

'I'm…all right.' He forced the words out and still didn't open his eyes. 'I see…something. Ships…they're attacking the city!' Tears started rolling down his cheeks as Alissa held him up. 'It's too late…the war has begun…'

Alissa looked up to the emperor whose hands were frozen in place while he stared at Japheth open-mouthed.

'Hey! Get those codes in! It's not too late to stop more from getting in!' As she spoke, she felt Japheth becoming limp in her arms. Looking down at him, she saw his eyes roll into the back of his head. 'Hey…don't you go anywhere.' Her voice had suddenly become soft.

Shem lifted Japheth over his shoulder and started walking towards the exit.

'Where are you taking him?'

'To Megan. If the fight really has started, then we're gonna need him.'

Alissa nodded. 'I'll keep the emperor safe. Be careful, Shem. You don't know what's out there.'

He nodded and disappeared out the door. Alissa turned back to the emperor. 'How much longer?' she demanded.

'I'm going as fast as I can!'

***

Ham rolled into the grease pit at the back of the workshop as the front wall exploded inwards. A shower of concrete scattered across the room. As the dust was settling, he peeked out the top and saw small fighter ships speeding past, shooting red lasers as they went.

He ducked back down into the pit and opened his comms pad. With shaking fingers, he called through to Alissa.

The moment her face filled the screen, Ham let his tears flow. 'Please help me.'

Alissa's face hardened for a moment, then seemed to melt in devastation. 'Ham? What's happening? Where are you?'

119

'In the workshop. There are ships out there, Alissa. They're firing on us.'

'Oh god…' Alissa closed her eyes. When she reopened them, Ham was still staring desperately at her. 'Okay, Ham. Stay exactly where you are. Don't let anyone see you. I'm on my way.'

He nodded while Alissa ended the comms and turned to the emperor. 'I'm sorry, but unless you're already finished…you're on your own.'

'I understand.' The emperor looked back down at the console. 'Go and save your friend.'

Alissa turned on her heel and ran out of the security facility.

***

When Shem arrived at the medical centre, Japheth was moving a little easier. 'I keep telling you, Shem, I'm fine. We should have stayed with Al.'

Shem didn't even look at him. 'She's better on her own.'

Japheth grabbed Shem's shirt weakly and tried to push him against the wall of the hospital. 'What the hell are you saying? That you abandoned her on purpose?'

Shem shook himself free. 'No…but she would risk her life to save one of us. If she's on her own then…'

Japheth relaxed his grip. 'We're not a burden to her, this way.'

Shem nodded. 'Come on. We find Megan, get you checked, then get on the front line.'

They ran to Megan's usual room. She was waddling around with a panicked look on her face and tears in her eyes as the men walked in.

'Meg? Are you okay?' Japheth took a step towards her.

'I'm fine. What's wrong?'

She ushered Japheth into a seat and started scanning him with a small handheld device. 'I had a vision, of the fighting. It was intense, and my head has been killing me since.'

Megan looked at the scanner readouts on a pad as she spoke. 'I can see why…there's a loss of synaptic function here.' Megan swapped her tools and cast a blue light emanating from a wand over Japheth's head. 'This should fix the problem. I would normally say avoid stress for a few days but…' Her voice trailed off as she glanced out the window to the city below.

A small portion was under attack. Not enough aggressive ships got in to cause citywide chaos and the vessels that were flying around were already under assault from ground troops, looking as though they wouldn't stay up much longer.

'We have to help the drovians.' Shem stared out the window as he spoke. 'They're only in danger because of us.'

'How did the committee even find us?'

Japheth looked over to Shem then back at Megan. 'Colfer.'

'Oh…' Megan paused then cried out in pain.

Shem and Japheth were by her side instantly. 'What's wrong? Are you all right?' Japheth put a supportive arm around her.

Megan nodded as Japheth eased her into a chair. 'I'm fine. It's just…' She looked between both of the men. 'I've been in labour for about an hour now…'

CHAPTER FIFTEEN

ALISSA RAN HARD AND FAST UNTIL SHE REACHED THE main doors of the security complex. She burst through to the outside and quickly surveyed her surroundings. It was a few miles back to the city, and while it was possible to run that far, it would take way too long.

There were a few vehicles parked in bays along the front of the building, but it was the hover cycle that caught her eye. It should be easy enough to hack start and would be faster than the bigger armoured trucks.

With deft fingers, Alissa opened the control panel of the bike and moved a few wires, then entered an override code she had learned in the workshop, which made the engine whir into life. She closed the panel, hopped onto the back, and revved the engine as she sped away towards the city.

It didn't take long before the rocky landscape turned into the familiar set of buildings and skyscrapers. Alissa powered through the streets towards the workshop. As she got closer, the destruction from the attack became clear. Buildings with burning holes blown into the sides, bodies littering the streets with paramedics working to save them, and crashed alien fighter ships smouldering on the road proved to be difficult to manoeuvre around, but Alissa wove in and out of the obstacles focussed on one objective—*save Ham.*

***

Japheth and Shem stood staring at Megan as she groaned her way through a contraction.

Japheth took her hand. 'What can we do?'

She looked at him with pleading eyes. 'Get out there and make sure my baby is born into a world that's safe.'

Shem stepped forward. 'We can't leave you—'

'Yes, you can!' she said, cutting him off. 'Shem, I've been through enough this year to know I am strong enough to have this baby on my own.' She groaned again. 'Please, stop the war and help save the city!'

Shem and Japheth looked at each other for a moment, both of them unmoving before Megan yelled, 'Both of you! Go!'

They both jumped into action and ran out the door leaving Megan to cope alone.

As they ran through the hospital, they saw the ramifications of the attack, both Drovians and Humans lining up with burns and gashes, some unconscious on beds waiting to be seen. The doctors and nurses rushing to triage. They could hear crying, low sobs escaping the mouths of victims who had lost people in the fight.

It bolstered both men, fuelled anger towards the Committee. They would pay for what they had done.

They ran out into the street, which was bustling with people clearing roads, helping the injured and dying, and putting out fires.

'Where do we go, Japheth?'

'The Guard house. It's not too far. We need weapons.'

They set off at a run. Within minutes, they saw a hoverbike hurtling round the corner with Alissa riding on the back.

Japheth spotted her first. 'Hey, Al!'

She glanced over and slowed the bike. 'I have to get to Ham.'

Shem's eyes widened. 'Why? What's happened? Is he okay?'

Alissa set her jaw. 'I don't know.'

Japheth glanced around them. 'The roads are pretty blocked from here. Even on the bike you'll struggle to get through. Where are you heading?'

'The workshop. It's only a few blocks from here.' Alissa climbed off the bike and let it fall to the ground. 'I guess we run from here.'

The three of them headed quickly towards the workshop. Alissa gasped audibly when they arrived. They entire front of the building had crumbled away. The bodies of the men that worked alongside her were strewn about. Medical staff were already here, trying to save those they could. Alissa carefully picked her way through the debris and called out for Ham.

At the back of the room came a quiet reply. 'Alissa?'

At the sound of his voice, both Shem and Alissa ran to where Ham hid. The grease pit was pretty well hidden by two sheets of metal and beneath them sat Ham, clutching his knees and crying.

Alissa dropped down and wrapped him in her arms. 'It's okay, Ham. I'm here now. I'm here.'

He released his knees and gripped Alissa tightly. 'I was so scared. Is it over now?'

'I don't think so. The city defences must've kicked in, but they'll still be out there, trying to breach them.'

Shem crouched down and looked over Ham. 'Are you hurt, man?

'No.'

'Okay, come on. We need to find somewhere safe.' Shem stood and pulled Ham up to his feet, giving him a quick hug. 'Megan's at the hospital, and she could probably use some help right about now. You think you can do that, Ham?'

He nodded. 'I think so.'

The four of them left the building and took Ham to Megan, who welcomed the help with open arms.

When she flinched and held her stomach, Ham gasped. 'Is your baby okay?'

She nodded and smiled. 'He's wonderful, but it seems like he's ready to come meet everyone.'

Alissa's face melted into a smile. 'Oh, Megan.' She wrapped her in a hug. 'Congratulations.'

'Thanks, now get out there and keep the city standing.'

Alissa nodded and headed to street level followed closely by Shem and Japheth. The three of them ran quickly to the Guard house and met with Garyx at the door. 'All right, kids. Assignments.'

He looked over to Japheth. 'You, take the girl and load yourselves up with weapons at the armoury.' Japheth nodded as Garyx turned to Shem. 'You a fighter?'

'Not really, I'm a navigation officer.'

'A flyer? Can you pilot the fighters?'

Shem nodded. 'Yeah, I think so.'

'Good.' Garyx marked something down on his pad. 'Get on this transport to the east dock. There are ships there. They'll assign you to one.' He pointed to a large black truck waiting at the other end of the street.

Alissa turned to Garyx. 'Wait, you can't separate us!'

Garyx raised his eyebrows and opened his mouth to speak, but Shem interrupted before he had chance. 'Come on, Al. I'm not one for hand to hand. You know that. But I might actually be able to help if I'm in the air.'

'But what if something happens?' Her voice was suddenly small.

Shem smiled. 'It won't. I'll see you when this is over.'

He wrapped her in a hug, and she whispered in his ear, 'Stay safe.'

Shem smiled then nodded at Japheth before running away from the group. Alissa felt a hand on her shoulder.

'Are you okay?'

She turned and looked up at Japheth. 'I'm fine.'

The armoury was situated in the basement of the guard house. Japheth led Alissa down to the room, and they stood with other humans and Drovians, awaiting weapons and instruction. The energy was high here, people waiting to fight for their homes, humans willing to protect this alien world with their lives.

They reached the front, and Alissa was handed a laser rifle. The Drovian woman handing out weapons looked at her. 'Have you ever used a weapon like this before?'

Alissa looked down at the gun in her hands. 'Yes.'

'Good.'

She was handed a backpack with extra energy clips, which she strapped on.

'All right, you two, you're on door duty. Get to the main outer hangar bay. If the committee breaches, that's where they'll do it.'

Alissa and Japheth nodded as the woman spoke. 'There's a transport heading there in four minutes. If you miss that, you're on foot.'

They nodded again and ran back to street level. Outside was an armoured vehicle with rows of seats inside. Alissa and Japheth jumped in just before they set off. She counted twelve people including herself and Japheth and hoped there would be more already there.

The journey was mostly silent and relatively short. Around five minutes before they arrived, a Drovian man stood at the front and looked at the faces of his fighters. 'It's on us. We are going to protect our homes with everything we have.' He looked stoic. Alissa watched him intently. 'The Committee destroyed our world once before, but we survived. Drovians always survive!'

The other people in the vehicle mumbled their agreement.

'Alongside our human friends, we will save our city!'

Again, everyone agreed but louder.

'We will not die today!'

The vehicle erupted in agreeing cheers.

He didn't believe what he was saying, that much Alissa could tell, but he was hyping up the fighters, and that's what they needed to get through this.

Once the vehicle stopped, Japheth and Alissa were the first ones out. They were pointed over towards a makeshift cover. Large steel crates filled with ship parts had been strategically placed around the hangar. Even with the large hangar bays sealed shut, Alissa could hear the sounds of explosions from other side. She ran across the hangar and dived behind a crate, followed quickly by Japheth.

Then they waited.

***

Shem hopped onto the transport. There were only a few people on board. He looked out the windows in time to see Alissa and Japheth charging inside the guard house. He turned back into his seat and waited. It took only a couple of minutes before Garyx hopped on board. 'Come on. Let's go.'

'You're going to the docks?' Shem looked confused. 'I thought you were assigning jobs?'

'I was. But I'm still one of the best to ever fly. I'm not letting this boat leave without me.'

129

It wasn't a long journey to the east docks, but there was no rousing speech for the pilots. They offloaded in silence and were pointed to their ships. Shem was given a single pilot fighter jet. He climbed up, seated himself inside, put on his helmet, and buckled in. It had been a long time since he'd truly piloted anything like this, but the mechanics were similar between Drovian and human consoles.

This would all come down to how well Shem could fly. He powered up the fighter and took to the air. The ships were modified to stop their altitude before they hit the rocky ceiling of the city. It was a relief to Shem, one less thing to worry about. He piloted the jet over towards the main hangar and positioned himself in formation with the other ships.

***

Ham watched the fighter jets whizz through the sky through the hospital window then turned back to Megan, who was sitting on a chair, leaning to the side and breathing heavily.

'They're all getting ready for the fight.'

'I know you want to help them, Ham.'

He bit at his bottom lip and looked at his hands. 'I do. But I'm too scared.'

Megan smiled kindly. 'I know, and it's okay. I need you here with me. I can't do this alone.'

Ham perked up slightly and puffed out his chest. 'Really? You need me?'

She nodded. 'Yeah, a human birth is a little different than a Drovian birth, and I can't deliver this baby without your help.'

Ham smiled and walked over to the chair where Megan sat. 'What can I do to help?'

***

Alissa gripped her gun tightly and glanced over at Japheth. His face was set in unbridled determination and his gaze never left the hangar bay doors. The explosions continued to ring out through the space, making Alissa feel uneasy about what was about to happen.

They had already started to buckle slightly. And Alissa could see the flash of lasers as they barraged against the doors.

'They've already penetrated the shields…' she murmured, and Japheth nodded. 'It won't be long now.'

He was right. It took around thirty minutes for the weapons to blow open a hole in the doors wide enough for fighter ships to fly through, and then a hoard of aliens stormed the hangar on foot.

Alissa crouched behind the crate as a volley of laser fire cut the air above her. She saw a Drovian cut down by it and squeezed her eyes shut for a moment. Then she heard Japheth's voice. 'Alissa! I need you to focus!'

With a deep breath, she turned back to the doors and aimed her rifle at the aliens on foot, blasting a group of them as they charged through the hangar. She watched as some of them crumpled to the ground, which caught the attention of their friends. They opened fire on Alissa who ducked for cover back behind the crate. She could hear the sounds of screams and laser fire echoing through the open room.

Japheth looked over to her. 'You okay?'

She nodded, and as the lasers against the crate stopped, Alissa and Japheth popped back up to open fire once more.

***

Shem held the jet in position as the hangar doors breached and all hell broke loose. Three alien jets flew into the city and opened fire. Two of them opened fire on the Drovian ships while one set to blasting the city below. Shem turned his weapons on that one and started shooting, tailing the jet as it flew over the buildings below. He was relentless in his anger as he fired upon the intruder, intent on destroying it before it killed too many people.

It didn't take long before he blasted through the ships armour, focusing his fire on the fuel sector. Within seconds of the concentrated fire, the ship exploded.

Shem turned the jet back towards the doors and saw another ten enemy ships had arrived. He charged into the fight.

***

Alissa pinned an alien to the ground with one arm and hit it in the face with the laser rifle. Her clip had emptied, and she hadn't been able to reload under the constant attack. She grunted as she hit him again, and he went limp in her grasp, giving her valuable seconds to catch her breath and pull another clip from her pack.

Just as she got her gun loaded, an alien leapt over the top of the crate, landing on Japheth just as Alissa turned and shot it dead.

'Thanks, Al.'

Alissa felt a half smile cross her face. 'Anytime.'

She turned back to the hangar doors. The aliens weren't relenting. They were pouring through into the city. 'We're running out of time.'

Japheth turned to look at her. 'What do you mean?'

'If we can't stop them, they'll overwhelm the city.'

'So what do we do?'

Alissa thought for a moment. 'I have to get onto their ship.'

Japheth fired a few shots into the fight then looked at Alissa. 'No way.'

'I have to. If there's a way to stop this, it's on that ship. I owe it to every person here to try.'

'You know I'm not gonna let you go alone.'

Alissa smiled slightly. 'I thought as much.'

'So how do we do it? How do we get up there?'

Alissa's smile disappeared. 'We need a pilot.'

**

Shem hit a corkscrew manoeuvre to avoid a laser barrage and just about righted himself before flying straight into one of the hotel towers. He looked at the carnage in the skies—fighter ships, both alien and Drovian, being shot out of the air, debris hitting the streets below. It was horrifying. Shem knew this could all be over for him at any moment, and he was riding high on that adrenaline.

His comms bleeped in his ear while he flew and auto-connected to the caller. 'Not really a good time…' Shem turned sharply and barrel-rolled away from another attack.

'Shem? It's Alissa.' She sounded worried, and rightly so given how their day had gone so far.

'What do you need, Al?'

'We need to get off the planet. Japheth and I are going to the mothership.'

His heart sank. 'What? They'll kill you before you ever get there!'

'Not if we have you to fly us up.'

'Al, you gotta be kidding with this.' He hoped she would hear the insanity of her plan and change her mind.

'Can you meet us in the town square?'

Shem sighed heavily. 'Sure Al. Give me ten minutes.'

***

'Okay, Shem's in. Now we just have to get across the city in one piece.' Alissa tossed the comms pad into her bag and checked her ammo. 'I've got one clip left.'

Japheth looked into his own. 'I'm on one.'

'Then we'd better be careful.'

The two of them snuck around the outer edge of the room, avoiding as much contact with the invading force as possible. There were doors along the side wall they were skirting, and

Alissa pressed the keypads as she went past. They all seemed to be locked down. She let out a frustrated sigh. 'We can't go out the main doors to the city—we'd be flattened by the aliens! How do we get out of here?'

Japheth tried the nearest keypad. 'Looks like an autolock. If we bypass it, it opens all the doors in here.'

Alissa glanced round. There were alien attackers banging on windowed rooms filled with Drovians and humans. 'If we do that, a lot of people are gonna die. We need to find another way.'

**

Shem landed heavily in a quiet alleyway. He had eluded the aliens and was for the time being hidden. He looked over at the fighter he'd been flying. There was no way that thing would make it to space. 'I need to find another ship.'

Suddenly realising he was now weaponless, Shem carefully made his way out of the alley and onto the street. The fight hadn't made it this far yet, so he slowly stalked through the city.

He watched the sky above him as jets battered each other with laser fire and an idea began to form in his head. He opened a channel to one of the Drovian pilots. 'Hey, it's Shem. Do you think you can take out the pilots of an invader without too much damage to the ship?'

The reply was a deep voice saying, 'You're asking a lot here.'

'I know, Garyx. But Alissa has a plan, and I need one of those ships.'

Shem heard the sound of a deep sigh. 'All right, but I can't guarantee a good landing.'

The comms clicked out, and Shem watched the skies carefully, trying to spot Garyx's ship. It was difficult, but he eventually spotted it, leading an invader away from the fray, lower and lower towards ground level. Shem leapt back as both ships flew past him almost driving along the street itself, until Garyx suddenly looped up and over. Shem watched open-mouthed as Garyx's cockpit opened and he shot three laser rounds directly into the skull of the main pilot.

The invading ship lost control and skidded the remaining few feet to the concrete, sparks flying as it ground to a slow stop.

Shem watched as Garyx landed his jet and jumped out of the cockpit. Still holding his gun, he approached the alien ship. Two creatures climbed down, looking panicked before more laser bolts flew through their craniums. They flopped dead onto the floor. Shem stared at Garyx with a mix of shock and awe. 'That was incredible!'

'Yeah, yeah. Told you I was the best. Here.' Garyx held out his gun. 'If you're planning on going up there, you're gonna need this.'

'Thanks!' Shem took the weapon gratefully and ran towards the alien ship.

It was difficult to drag the dead pilot from his seat but not impossible. He hit the ground with a sickening crack. Shem tried his best to ignore it and jumped into the pilot seat. 'Okay, let's see how you fly.'

The comms clicked in his ear. It was Garyx again. 'Attention all flyers, we have a human-controlled enemy ship heading into the skies. Do not fire. Repeat…Do. Not. Fire.'

Shem smiled and gently took his new ship into the skies.

***

'We're running out of time, Japheth.' Alissa looked around the bay wildly. 'We need to get to Shem.'

As the words passed her lips, the sound of metal hitting metal came echoing from the city doors. Alissa whirled round in time to see one of the alien ships come crashing through, smearing a line of foot soldier intruders as it skidded to a halt. The hatch opened up, and Shem's worried face scanned the room.

The drovians took the opportunity to reposition themselves defensively once more as Alissa and Japheth ran full speed towards the ship. Alissa's eyes were wide as she looked over the vessel. 'Shem! How did you get this?'

He smiled in return. 'Long story. Can you get the shields back up on this thing?'

Alissa climbed into the vessel and looked around. 'I should think so…why?'

'Well, the original pilot was shot through the hatch so we've got a hole.'

Alissa took a deep breath and nodded while Japheth climbed in as well. Shem closed the hatch and engaged the engines. 'It's gonna take around thirteen minutes to reach upper atmo in this thing. That's all the time you'll have, Al.'

'Right' was the only answer she could give. This was her idea, her plan, and she had to make sure it worked. She opened a panel at the back of the cockpit and started working.

Japheth took the seat next to Shem and looked at the controls. 'What can I do?'

'Take tactical. Don't shoot unless they do but scan any ship we pass for weak spots. We might find ourselves in a heap of trouble here.'

Japheth nodded and started to familiarise himself with the controls as Shem powered through the hangar bay doors and out into the desert.

While Alissa pressed buttons and worked on the shielding, her mind wandered to Ham. They had left him behind. She suddenly felt a pang of guilt at the thought of him finding out she had died alongside Shem. She pulled her comms pad out of her pocket and called through to him.

Ham answered pretty quickly and smiled at Alissa while she worked. She had set the comms on the small shelf next to where she was working and smiled back as she saw his beaming face. 'Hey, Ham, how's it going?' Shem turned in his seat to glance back when he heard her talk.

'Hey, Al, it's going well. Megan says the labour is going right.'

'That's great news, Ham.' Alissa continued to connect wires to bypass the shields' drained power cells.

'Where are you, Al?'

She hesitated. 'I'm…on my way to the mothership. With Japheth…and Shem.'

Ham's mouth hung open and his eyebrows almost met in the middle. 'But…what if you die?'

'I won't.' Alissa heard a slight hum as the shields kicked in.

'But you might—you can't say that. You don't know!'

Alissa heard Megan's voice from in the room somewhere. 'Ham, it's all right.'

'No! You should have taken me with you!'

'Ham, I love you so much. You know that, right?' She could see him blinking back tears.

'I know,' he replied in a quiet voice.

Alissa stood and moved to the front of the ship holding the comms pad in front of Shem.

'I'm sorry, man.'

'Please, don't leave me alone. I don't want to do that again.'

Alissa swallowed the lump forming in her throat. 'You won't. I'm coming back, Ham. I promise you. I'm coming back.'

CHAPTER SIXTEEN

THE EMPEROR STOOD AT THE WINDOW OF THE TOP floor in the tallest building his city had to offer, looking out on the battle below. He was getting updates reported through every ten minutes or so.

We've lost another jet, their forces are breaking through, they've taken the hangar, casualty report...casualty report...casualty report...

He shook his head, his face stoic. If they didn't do something drastic, the city would be lost in a matter of hours. He made the decision to evacuate the city.

The alert system that was designed for the Drovians was simple yet effective. It would send an alert to the comms of every citizen, directing them to the Through and Through. They would take refuge in their sister city and collapse the tunnel. It would take the Committee days to find them, which would allow them to set up full defences and prepare.

His eyes welled up and a tear slid down his cheek as he turned away from the window and entered his command codes into the communication array.

***

'We're breaking atmo. Let's hope the shield holds.' Shem looked worried as the sky above them darkened into blackness.

The ships they had passed on the way had mostly ignored them, leaving them all breathing a sigh of relief.

'So, what now?' Japheth's voice was calm, and he never took his eyes off the vast ship hanging above the planet as they approached.

'We could probably land in the docking bays, but the minute we get out…'

'We'd get shot.' Alissa finished Shem's thought. 'Scan the surface of the ship—are there any external airlocks or emergency bays that might be unmanned?'

Japheth's fingers moved deftly over the console as he completed his scans. 'There's a few that don't have life signs in the immediate area. But that doesn't mean it won't change by the time we've docked.'

Alissa nodded. 'We're gonna have to risk it.' She cocked her laser rifle.

Shem glanced up at her as she did. It struck him then, for the first time really, how different she really was. For just a moment, she felt like a stranger to him.

He shook the feeling away and programmed the docking sequence for the ship, sending through the small vessel's authorisation codes as protocol.

The ship aligned with an airlock off the port and slowly connected its umbilical tunnel. Alissa stood at the door, gun in hand, and waited. Japheth stood beside her, and as the ship juddered slightly to announce the solid connection, Shem joined them.

The door slid back with a woosh of air. The pressure was changed slightly causing Alissa's ears to pop. She crossed the short tunnel and opened the airlock hatch. Quickly the three of them slipped inside and looked through the airlock door to the corridors ahead. They were clear.

They entered the ship proper, quietly made their way down the corridor, and then ducked through an open door into what appeared to be empty quarters. They locked the door behind them and breathed for what seemed like the first time in an eternity. Shem looked to Alissa. 'All right, we're here. What's the plan?'

'Destroy the ship.'

'Okay…so, how do we do that?'

Alissa opened her mouth to speak but paused. Shem shifted his footing slightly and raised an eyebrow. 'Al, please tell me you have an idea of how to do that.'

'Well, not a complete idea.'

Shem's hands came up to his face, and he inhaled deeply, before turning on his friend. 'Are you kidding me? We are literally standing in enemy territory and you're telling me we don't have a plan! Are you trying to get us killed?'

Japheth took a step between Shem and Alissa. 'Hey, calm down, man. Let's think about this.'

The room fell silent as Shem turned his back to the others and began pacing. Alissa watched him as he did, and Japheth stood beside her. 'Okay, what about using the mainframe in engineering? Like Ham did last time.'

Alissa looked at him. 'What?'

Shem turned to face them again. 'On the last Committee ship, remember? Ham did something in engineering that overloaded the engines and destroyed the ship.'

'Okay…how do we get to engineering?'

'It won't be easy. We're gonna have to fight our way through.'

Alissa looked down at her feet. 'I'm sorry, Shem. I shouldn't have brought you up here.'

'It was my choice, Alissa. Not yours.' He made his way to the door. 'Okay, ready?'

Alissa and Japheth both raised their guns and nodded. Shem pressed the keypad and the doors slid open. The two with guns ran through and surveyed the immediate corridors. Japheth called back. 'We're clear. Come on, Shem.'

The three of them moved slowly, checking every corner, listening for any sound. They had moved about halfway across the deck when they heard conversations coming from in front of them. Alissa held up her hand and motioned the group to go back. The corridor they had come down was a long and empty one. The voices were too close. Japheth shook his head at her gently and raised his gun. Alissa looked at him then did the same.

As the two guards stepped around the corner, they were immediately shot by the humans and fell dead to the ground.

Alissa took their pistols and handed Shem her rifle. 'You okay with taking this?'

Shem looked at the weapon in his hands. 'Do I have a choice?'

Alissa smiled weakly. 'I don't think you do. I'm sorry.'

***

Colfer sat on the cold metal floor of his cell, knees wedged up to his chin and hugging his legs for warmth. He shivered anyway. The cell was mostly dark, just a low level light emanating from a strip along the top of the wall. There was no furniture in this room, just Colfer, sitting on the floor.

His head ached from the alien onslaught he had experienced during his interrogation with Xyan. And he realised very quickly that if he protected Alissa, he would be killed for it. Would that make amends for the death sentence he cast upon her? Probably not. For hours he pondered whether she had made the right choices on board The Ark. Taking a ship to the Committee, saving Japheth, blowing their ship up…

They were going to find us eventually.

It came with the realisation that the Committee were responsible for the captain being killed. He began to think that had he been in Alissa's shoes, he might have made some of the same decisions.

But it was too late now. His only choice was betray her and save himself, or protect her and die. He gingerly touched the open gash on his forehead and winced. This wasn't fair.

He was pondering his choices when he heard a bleep coming from the door sensor and it slid open to reveal a blue-skinned alien, small in stature but heavy in brow. He stepped inside and closed the door behind him.

Colfer attempted to stand up to face the creature, but a blue hand rested gently on his shoulder. 'Please, stay where you are. I don't have much time, and I need you to listen very carefully.'

The blue alien crouched down to the ground in front of Colfer. 'I need your help.'

Colfer shook his head. 'No way…I'm not telling you where she is.'

A look of confusion spread across the blue face. 'What? Who?'

'Alissa. I'm not telling you anything about her.'

'My friend, I don't know what you're talking about.'

Colfer's eyes met the alien's. 'Then what do you want?'

'I want to stop Xyan from destroying the planet.'

'I don't understand…'

'My name is Kreven. I am a science officer on board this ship and a member of Project Black.'

Colfer shifted his position slightly to take pressure off his aching hip. 'What's Project Black?'

'Centuries ago, the civilisations that had made their way into space greeted each other warmly, at peace with the knowledge that they were not alone. My race was the first to offer unification.'

Colfer listened carefully, trying to follow Kreven's words.

'They created the Interplanetary Collective. A council represented by high-ranking leaders from all joined planets. All

145

seemed well, and they governed trade routes, introduced new races to interstellar travel, and created a peaceful universe.'

'So what went wrong?'

Kreven laughed bitterly. 'Life. You see, up until that point, space had been explored only by the races that had advanced far enough to create the technology, races that focussed on peace and unity. Until the Coleoptera, that is. They cared only for war. The dominant continent on their world had won the battle for control and exterminated those around them. Leaving a world dominated by like-minded beings.

'They travelled into space and began their wars. But they were outnumbered in the end. Forced back to their own world.'

Colfer frowned. 'So they gave your people a taste of war?'

'Yes.' Kreven nodded. 'And my people did not care for it. However, they understood that not all races would share their desire for unity. So they created Project Black. A secret fleet of ships were created and manned by hand-chosen representatives from various United planets. They created the Committee to oversee the project and ensure they stayed within their limits.'

'So...what changed?'

'The project's main task was to eradicate potential threats before they made it into space. That mostly meant targeting space centres on planets that were deemed too dangerous. They would spend years watching and researching worlds before they took action. And when they did, it was surgical in its precision—minimal casualties and a safer universe for the United Collective, until the Drovian incident.'

Colfer was listening intently, hanging on every word spoken.

'The planet below us was deemed too dangerous for space travel thanks to a war they fought over five hundred years prior. A few people in the project disagreed. The Drovians had lived in peace for half a century, but that wasn't enough for the general responsible. He destroyed key points of the city as expected, but failed to register their combustible power sources. The planet was destroyed in days. It was assumed that all life had been eradicated. It was decided then that genocide was too high a risk to continue operating the same way.

'It was decreed by the Unified Collective that all Project Black tasks must be undertaken in secret. No planet could ever find out that they were being kept from space. I believe that was the case with your own. Your ships were only destroyed if they left your solar system, leaving no trace. Humanity would never have known the truth.'

Colfer's face twisted in anger. 'Our planet was dying! Those Arks were humanity's only chance.'

'We know. That was my first indication that the Committee was not following the rules laid before them. The general on board this ship enjoys the violence and power Project Black brings him. He has campaigned multiple times to bring back the old ways, found settlements of surviving Coleoptera, and brought them onto his ship to serve.'

'Wait…they're the insect-looking creatures.'

Kreven nodded. 'I suppose they would appear that way to you, yes.'

'Once Xyan realised the Drovians had not only survived, but were thriving *and* helping the humans, he lost what little control he had left.'

147

'I don't think it helped that his wife's ship was the one we destroyed.'

'There are those of us on board this ship, Colfer, that want to end this madness once and for all. We want to show the corruption within the ranks of the Committee and put an end to Project Black.'

'How?'

Kreven smiled. 'My friend…that's where you come in.'

CHAPTER SEVENTEEN

ALISSA SLOWLY PICKED HER WAY ALONG A CORRIDOR, reaching the junction at the end and glancing quickly both ways. There were groups of guards coming from both sides. There wasn't much time. She silently moved along the metallic corridor back to her friends and pressed her back against the wall. They were mostly hidden by a bulkhead and would only be seen if someone came right past them.

She focussed so hard on listening for what was in front that she almost missed the sound of footsteps coming from the other end of the corridor. Whipping her head around, she saw three security-looking types. Bipedal insectoids. They were being pinned in and the guards hadn't even realised. If there was ever a time to make the first move, it was now. Alissa stepped out onto the middle of the corridor and pointed a gun at each group. She pulled the trigger, and the first two guards fell.

Within seconds, the other guards were pulling up their guns and taking aim. Alissa ran to the insectoid guards while Shem and Japheth covered her by shooting at the other group. She shot as she ran, managing to hit one guard while dodging the fire from the others. Her body had taken over, was running on muscle memory alone.

Japheth took down three of the blue-skinned guards while the remaining six were taking cover at the junction end of the corridor. Shem fired wildly in the direction of the guards, offering cover fire but not precise enough to take anyone out.

Alissa reached the insectoids and pistol-whipped one across the face. There was a crunch as the butt of the gun cracked into the exoskeleton, leaving a dented shell, oozing with yellow goo. The guard looked at her with wild eyes, attempting to fire his gun at point-blank range. Alissa wrapped her arms around his weapon and spun around, pointing it directly at the other guard as the trigger was pulled. She heard the thud as he fell to the ground, and she flipped the weapon to aim at his own face and shot.

With haste, Alissa flung herself back at the wall to avoid the firing from the end of the corridor. Checking the charge on her weapons made Alissa frown. She dropped to the ground and grabbed the weapons from the fallen insect guards. Then she looped the straps over her shoulders and allowed the guns to hang down her back.

She settled herself on the ground on her stomach, behind the insect guards, and pulled a laser rifle to her eye. Carefully she waited until a blue-skinned guard poked his head out. She hit him between the eyes.

Soon all the guards had fallen and the three friends grouped back together. Alissa inspected the group. 'All right, injuries?'

'None.' Shem shook his head. Japheth looked Alissa up and down. There was no blood showing. 'You came out of that unscathed?'

'Yeah.' A look of embarrassment spread across her face. She had never unleashed herself like that in front of them, and the look on Shem's face told her everything she needed to know. He was afraid of her.

***

'You want me to do what?' Colfer stood in his cell face-to-face with Kreven.

'I want you to break into the system and send a priority message to the Unified Collective.'

'No! No way…why can't you do it?'

Kreven looked at his feet. 'Because when the message is received, there's going to be a lot of trouble on this ship. I need to be ready for the fight.'

'What do you mean?' Colfer gripped the comms pad tightly that Kreven had handed him.

'The general here has a lot of friends on board that agree not only with his actions, but with his motives as well. They will stand by him regardless of the orders from the Collective.' Kreven handed Colfer a small laser pistol. 'Use the codes on the pad and keep safe, my friend. We're counting on you.'

Kreven turned and left the cell, leaving the door unlocked. He had already given Colfer a detailed map of the ship's internal venting system, a safe route to travel without being caught by the guards. With a deep, steadying breath, Colfer left the confines of his cell.

***

Alissa, Shem, and Japheth were running. There was a parade of guards on their tail, and with each corridor they passed, more appeared, keeping them pinned. At random hallways, guards would appear out of nowhere, leaving them to take sharp turns. Alissa had lost track completely of their destination and was just trying to stay alive.

'Why aren't they shooting at us?' Shem shouted as they ran.

'Just be grateful' was all Japheth could manage.

Alissa thought had about that question. Why weren't they shooting? With the long stretches of corridor, the guards would have easy shots. And yet here they were, still alive and still running. Yet more and more guards arrived. 'They don't want us dead.' Alissa began to slow. 'They're pinning us in. They want to take us alive.' And with that, Alissa stopped running and turned to face the guards behind her. There were over twenty of them now, all with weapons pointing at her. On the other side came even more.

'Drop your weapons, humans!'

Alissa looked to Shem and Japheth, then nodded, dropping her own pistols and the rifles on her back. She turned back to the guard that spoke. 'All right. What now?'

'You come with us.'

They were quickly surrounded and marched down the halls of the ship, surrounded by a mix of alien creatures, the blue skins and the insects.

***

Ham grimaced as Megan squeezed his hand through a contraction. After a few seconds, she glanced up at her friend, and after seeing his expression, she quickly released her vicelike grip. 'Oh, Ham, I'm sorry.'

He smiled. 'No, it's okay! You can squeeze my hand if you need to. It's doesn't hurt much.'

'It'll be a few minutes before I need to.' She lay back against the pillows on the bed.

'Do you need some water? Or some food?'

Megan smiled. 'No, honey, I'm all right.'

Ham nodded and picked her hand back up in his, almost as if he wanted to arm wrestle. 'Okay, I'm ready.'

Megan laughed as the monitor on the wall clicked into life.

'Drovians and humans alike. The city is lost.' The emperor's face filled the screen. His eyes were glassy and he looked so tired. Megan gasped as he spoke, and her free hand flew to her mouth. 'No…'

'All survivors must now evacuate via the Through and Through. Please make your way there quickly and efficiently. Help your neighbours and flee to safety. We will seal the tunnel in exactly two hours.'

With that, the screen went dark.

153

Megan sat, open-mouthed looking at the blank screen when another contraction ripped through her. She squeezed Ham's hand, and once more he grimaced. It took a couple of minutes, but soon Megan was relaxing as the pain eased. Ham looked down at her. 'What did the emperor mean?'

Megan was breathing heavily as she replied, 'It means we have to get across the city and onto the T&T.'

'Can you do that?' Ham looked concerned as Megan tried to pull herself up to her feet.

'I don't know. But what choice do we have?'

Ham reached out and helped Megan walk across the room. She held her belly as she walked, praying that the baby wouldn't arrive before they were safe.

Her legs buckled under the pain of another contraction. They were coming too fast. The baby was coming now.

Ham helped her back to the bed and stood vigilantly by her bedside. Megan shook her head. 'Ham, you need to get out of here. They're evacuating the city.'

'I can't. No one will be here to help you. If I go, you'll be all alone.'

Megan blinked back tears, and she tried to breathe through the pain. 'Ham, please…'

Ham sat in the chair beside the bed. 'I'm staying, Megan.'

***

Alissa walked quickly, surrounded by guns pointing in her direction. The hallways all looked the same, and she had no idea where they might be. She glanced at Shem. He was visibly nervous, his eyes wide, and he was trying hard to keep his face set in a stony glare. On her other side walked Japheth. He looked more relaxed. It wasn't the first time he had found himself captured by these beings, and he looked more angry than afraid.

The guards led them through a large set of double sliding doors and into a room. It was tiered, with them standing on the higher point. Alissa took in her surroundings. Computer terminals lined the walls, in the centre of the room was a big chair on a small plinth, and on the far wall was a large viewscreen with an image of the Drovian home world.

Alissa slowed to take it all in and was quickly shoved from behind to keep her moving. They were walked in between the viewscreen and the large occupied chair. In it sat a blue-skinned alien. He was leaning to the side, his chin resting on his hand in a thoughtful pose. He watched carefully as the three humans were stopped in front of him.

The guards spread back, leaving the three humans standing in front of the general. He stared at Alissa for a long time, and she didn't break the eye contact. He was responsible for all this, and she hated him.

Eventually, he blinked slowly and sat up straight in the chair. 'You are Alissa Namaah?'

She nodded in response, and the alien pulled out a gun and levelled it at her head. 'I ought to kill you right here.'

Alissa inhaled deeply and stood up straight facing her death head-on. 'What's stopping you?'

'Alissa!' Shem hissed from beside her.

The general smiled slowly. 'Revenge.' He rose to his feet. He was impressively tall and wearing a black uniform. 'You were on board the Ik'Omeg, correct?'

155

Alissa nodded gently, still never taking her eyes off him.

'You met the general there?'

Again, she nodded but couldn't help opening her mouth. 'Friend of yours, was she?'

A foul grin spread across the blue face. 'She was my wife.'

'I've gotta tell you, I didn't much care for her.' Alissa smiled back.

'Oh, the attitude of the young. You've boarded my ship, killed members of my crew…you must be feeling quite pleased with yourself.'

Alissa shrugged. 'I'd be happier if we'd managed to destroy your ship.'

The general took a step towards her. 'Alissa, you destroyed my family. And now, I intend to return the favour.'

He looked over to the guards and nodded. They stepped forward, and two guards grabbed Alissa's arms. She watched helplessly as two guards grabbed Shem and forced him onto his knees, while another two did the same to Japheth.

'Now…you killed the person I value most in the universe and it's time I returned the favour.'

Alissa struggled against the guards holding her. 'What?'

'I'm going to kill one of them. But…the choice of who is yours.'

Alissa's mouth slowly fell open in horror as the general's words sank in. 'What? No!'

'I thought you may not be amenable to my request. However, I do believe I have an excellent incentive. Choose one human to die, right here. And I will stop the attack on the planet. The humans and Drovians will be given immunity from the Committee.'

Alissa shook her head. 'You're sick!'

The general flew at her, stopping mere inches from her face. 'Perhaps I am, but knowing that doesn't help you.'

Alissa looked at the men kneeling before her. She had known Shem for a big part of her adult life. All the days they ate together in the cafeteria, drank together in Saime's, or just hung out watching movies. He was her best friend, knew everything about her.

But then there was Japheth. They had literally shared their minds, been connected in a way that no other humans had ever experienced. He understood who she had become because he was there when she became it.

'Tick tock, Alissa. The longer you take, the more people die on the surface.'

'I can't…'

'You have to.' Japheth looked up at her. 'Look, you wanted to save the planet down there, and this is your chance. Let him kill me.'

Alissa shook her head and tears dripped from her eyes. 'Japheth, no.'

'Come on, Al. You know it's the right choice. How are you gonna tell Ham you came back with me instead of Shem?'

'Al…'

She turned to the voice. Shem was looking at the ground.

'This isn't about Ham. It's about you. And you don't need me anymore.'

Alissa looked back to the general. 'I'm not gonna choose.'

157

CHAPTER EIGHTEEN

THE VENTS WERE SMALL AND CRAMPED AND SMELLED faintly of ionised metal. Colfer pulled himself along on his stomach, pulling out the comms pad every few minutes to check he was still going the right way. The gun he now had felt heavy against his hip, reminding him with every movement that he might have to kill someone.

He gritted his teeth as he continued, sweating in the hot, uncomfortable tunnel. He didn't have much farther to go. Only another minute or two and he would reach the vent. His arms were exhausted, but he powered on, coming to find a vent along his left side. With tired hands, he unlatched the metal grate and let it fall to the floor.

The vent had run parallel to this corridor, and Colfer poked his head out to find he was at floor level. The corridor was empty, *as expected.* Clamouring to his feet, Colfer checked the weight of the gun against his hip and sighed. The door now facing him was the end game.

158

Slowly he fingered the keypad and the door slid open with a whoosh. He poked his head inside. The room was relatively small. Looked like an unused research lab with a few consoles along the back. With a hissing sound, the door closed behind him.

It took longer than he'd hoped to find where the disk would insert in a machine like this. Seemed like a silly thing to ask at the time but the pure frustration of failure nearly brought Colfer to tears. But eventually he found the slot and let the console pull the disk from his fingers. He watched the screen as it whirred quietly, loading the data.

Writing appeared on the screen: INPUT OVERRIDE CODES.

Colfer looked at the pad in his hand. Kreven had added all the codes he needed. All he had to do now was hope they worked.

Once the codes were fully inputted, Colfer froze. The last step was initializing the upload sequence. It was simple enough, would only take him a second, but he knew the minute he did it, he would be caught and probably killed. There was a reason Kreven and the other resistance members weren't willing to do this. It was ultimately a suicide mission.

He looked down at the comms pad once more. It had recording capability. He stared at it for a few minutes, contemplating what he was about to do. But he wanted something. A record to remain of why he did what he did. With a heavy heart, he started recording.

'I don't know who's gonna get this, be you human or alien, but my name is Daniel Colfer. I was a Chief Nav Officer on board The Ark before it was destroyed. I banished Alissa,

159

Shem, and…Ham to die in the desert. I helped the Committee find the city.' He paused for a moment. It hurt him to admit what he had done. 'I see the bigger picture now, and I'm trying to do my part to make things right…I'm sorry.'

***

'My patience is wearing thin, Alissa.' The general paced behind her. 'Choose.'

She looked at the two men on their knees. 'Please don't make me do this.'

As she looked down at her friends, a guard approached the general and whispered in his ear. She watched his face change from stoic to slightly amused. His eyebrows raised, and he chuckled slightly. 'Oh…that's perfect.'

He took a step towards Alissa. 'It appears we may have something of interest to you.' He gestured to the viewscreen, which flickered from the view of the planet to an image of a research lab.

Alissa squinted at the figure on the screen, tucking a comms pad into his belt. 'Colfer?'

Japheth and Shem tried to turn their heads to look at the screen behind them, but the guards held them firmly in place, until the general smiled. 'Let the humans see their friend.'

'He's no friend,' growled Japheth.

The general nodded. 'A sentiment we unfortunately share.'

'You mean he's not helping you?'

The general looked back over to Alissa. 'He was, albeit without realising it. Once he knew who we truly were, he was no longer inclined to follow instruction.'

160

'So, what is he doing?'

The general kept smiling. 'I don't know. But it doesn't matter anyway.' He nodded, and suddenly the door to the lab opened. A guard walked in, gun aimed at Colfer. There was no sound with the feed so they all watched in silence as the guard yelled at Colfer. His eyes widened, and he quickly turned to the console as the guard raised his gun.

'Danny!' The scream came from Alissa as a blast hit Colfer in the back and he fell over the terminal then slid unmoving to the floor. The viewscreen cut back to the planet view while Alissa stared in horror.

'You bastards!' Shem struggled against the guards. 'You're nothing without your men behind you!'

The general looked to Shem. 'You have a lot to say for someone in your position.'

'You have no idea,' Shem growled. 'This ridiculous game is over. Alissa didn't kill your wife.'

Japheth's eyes widened. 'Shem…don't…'

The general moved closer. 'I beg your pardon?'

'I said, Alissa didn't kill your wife. I did. I smashed her skull with the butt of my gun, and I'd do it again.'

'Shem, no…' Alissa felt dread deep in the pit of her stomach. It felt like her skin had just turned to ice as she watched the general press the barrel of the laser pistol against Shem's temple.

'You are running out of time, Alissa. I may just have to choose for you.'

'No!' She struggled against the guards. 'Please…it's still my fault. He did it to save me. Blame me!'

161

***

Daniel Colfer coughed, and his mouth filled with the taste of blood. The floor was hard beneath him and felt like it was drawing the heat out of him. Daniel Colfer was cold.

He looked up, and the guard was now facing the door, waiting for more to come he supposed. He wanted to move, he wanted to get up and run, but his legs were so cold, he could barely tell they were there.

I'm dying.

His hand rested over his midsection, and he could feel the smooth casing of the gun he had against his fingertips. Slowly and carefully, he wrapped his hand around it and pulled it up to his face. Looking carefully down the barrel, he pointed it at the back of the alien's head and pulled the trigger.

The guard fell, and Colfer let the gun slip from his grasp. There was still time. He still had a chance. Eyeing up the console, he let out a low moan. It seemed so high, impossible to reach from the floor. With everything he had left, Colfer reached his hand up and grasped the console. He pulled himself painfully up to his knees, his eyes just peering over the edge.

The sequence was programmed. It just needed activating. Just one button. But which one? Colfer shook his head, and it rang in agony. His brain was getting fuzzier.

Which one!!!

He could feel the darkness creeping into his vision. This was it. He thrust his hand down and pressed the console pad as his vision faded to black.

Colfer slipped back to the floor, eyes staring at the wall, unblinking, unmoving. Colfer was dead.

***

CHAPTER NINETEEN

'BREATHE, MEGAN!' HAM'S VOICE WAS PANICKED AS HE ran through the hospital pushing his friend in a wheelchair. The whole place was empty. Abandoned. They had evacuated the hospitals in the city first, but Megan had insisted on staying to have her baby. But she realised when it was too late that the baby wasn't coming quite yet.

She couldn't walk. She could barely think, but Ham had taken control and carried her to the chair so he could try to get her to safety.

They reached street level quickly, and Ham pushed Megan onto the sidewalk. 'Which way do we go?'

She looked around—there was carnage everywhere. In the distance the sounds of laser fire and explosions rang out.

'Left. Go left and follow the road. It should lead us to the T&T.'

Ham nodded and began carefully pushing Megan's chair through the debris littering the city. She squealed as pain ripped through her.

'Sorry! I'm sorry!'

'It's all right, Ham. Keep going!'

They took a corner so sharply that the chair almost toppled over, but Ham managed to keep it steady.

They found themselves faced with five aliens pointing guns at them. 'Oh god!' Megan closed her eyes and wrapped her arms around her bump as Ham halted the chair. He ran around her and stood between Megan and the soldiers.

'You can't hurt her. I won't let you.'

One of the soldiers looked down at a comms pad in his hand. 'Humans. They're kill targets.'

Ham flinched as they spoke but stood his ground between the guns and Megan. 'I won't let you. I'll stop you.' He felt a hand intertwine with his own and looked down at Megan, who blinked back tears.

'It's all right, Ham. You did everything you could.'

The soldiers raised their guns.

***

An alarm blared, making Alissa flinch slightly. The general's eyes widened, and his mouth twisted, baring his teeth. He turned away from Shem, allowing the gun to lower enough that his life was no longer in immediate danger.

The general marched across the room to one of the men and a terminal against the wall. 'What's going on?'

The worker shook his head. 'I don't know, sir. We're locked out of all the systems.'

The general turned back to Alissa, pointing the gun at her. 'What did you do?'

'Nothing.' She shook her head. 'You've had us trapped in here, remember?'

He growled again and stepped closer to Alissa. 'Fine, your usefulness has come to an end.'

He levelled the gun at her face. 'Goodbye, Alissa.'

Suddenly, the room went dark, but within seconds, it was lit once more, albeit dimly.

'Sir, we're down to emergency power.'

The general turned to the worker again. 'Find out what the Hell is going on!'

'Sir, there's an incoming transmission.'

'Well, play it!'

An automated voice rang out through the ship. 'Project Black is terminated. Return immediately to the Committee. General Xyan must be apprehended. Open channel eight seven three three two.'

For one brief moment, Alissa felt the guards hold on her arms waver slightly and she took her chance. Pulling one arm free, she used it to flip the other guard. She grabbed his gun and pointed it at the general. 'Everyone stop or I shoot your boss!'

The room froze, all except for the general who slowly turned to face Alissa. 'This will not be tolerated, human.' He looked to the men standing around him. 'Shoot them!'

Silence. The guards didn't raise their guns.

Alissa stared into Xyan's eyes. 'It's over. You're done.'

Before Alissa could speak again, the viewscreen flashed and a woman filled the screen. Blue-skinned and heavy browed, she was a member of Xyan's race. One of the workers turned from his terminal. 'Channel eight seven three three two open, sir.'

Xyan turned once more to the screen, almost cowering beneath the harsh gaze of the woman. 'President! What a pleasant surprise!'

'General Xyan, we've received documented evidence that the Drovians survived the genocide incident. Is that correct?'

'Yes, it is!' Alissa stepped forward.

The guards holding Shem and Japheth had loosened their grip on them, and both now stood beside Alissa.

The president looked down at the three humans. 'You are the human species, is that correct?'

Alissa nodded, and the woman continued. 'Project Black has worked on its own initiative for many years now with no need for intervention from us. I see now that this was a mistake.'

Alissa stood looking up at the viewscreen. 'What's going on?'

'Project Black was a peace-keeping operation to ensure the safety of peaceful space-faring races. Eliminating the threat of violent races reaching space.'

'And you were okay with that?' Japheth spoke up. 'You were okay with them murdering innocent people?'

The president sighed. 'The old ways of genocide were tossed aside after the attack on the Drovian Empire. But it seems the general here and a few other dissidents decided to work off their own agendas.'

Shem stepped forward. 'They tried to stop us. What's so wrong with humanity.'

'Centuries ago your race was obsessed with warmongering. You were considered a potential threat. Project Black was to monitor your progress and feedback. They took matters into their own hands. For that, and the lives you have lost, I am sorry.'

'So what happens now?' Alissa kept her voice calm.

'You're free to live out your lives with the remainder of the Drovian Empire. You'll have no more to fear from the Committee. Guards, take Xyan into custody.'

Alissa turned to watch but quickly realised Xyan was gone. 'What? Where is he?'

'That way!' Japheth pointed to the door and bolted towards it.

The guards followed closely behind. Alissa turned to run when she heard the president's voice once more. 'Wait…'

She stopped and turned. 'What do you want?'

'The general isn't alone in his beliefs. He has handpicked his crew, including the Coleoptera. A vicious race that will not turn against Xyan. I'm sorry, but the ship you stand on has just become a war zone.'

CHAPTER TWENTY

THE SOLDIERS LOWERED THEIR GUNS. MEGAN OPENED   her eyes and saw the moment they stood down. 'What's going on?'

One of the men stepped forward. 'New orders from the Committee. The war is over.'

Megan almost laughed before a powerful contraction ripped through her abdomen. 'Ham!' She squeezed his hand as he knelt beside her.

'It's all right. I'm here.' He turned to the soldiers. 'Please help me get her back to the hospital!'

The men looked at each other then back to Ham. 'All right.'

***

Japheth ran through the corridors. He was close behind Xyan and getting closer by the second. He whirled round the

169

corner and came face-to-face with the insectoids. There were six of them, fully armed, and they opened fire. Japheth hit the ground and rolled out of the line of fire, pressing his back against the wall. Coming up behind him were more of the blue-skinned guards. The one at the front called out to Japheth, 'We can give you cover fire. Stop the general!'

Japheth nodded, and the guards flooded the corridor, shooting at the insectoids. They had opened the attacking line up enough that Japheth could get through unscathed as they hid from the laser fire.

He carried on after Xyan. His heart was pumping as fast as his legs. Fights were breaking out all through the ship, blue skins fighting the insectoid race. Japheth found himself having to duck and dodge errant shots that almost hit him.

There was a moment where he threw himself to the ground behind a half wall in a room full of the insectoids firing in his direction. Japheth looked around wildly, hoping to see something he could use to get him out of this.

Seconds later, he heard more laser fire from the door he came in. Sneaking a quick look, he saw Alissa and Shem, both holding laser rifles and firing at the guards.

Alissa caught his eye. 'Run!'

Japheth nodded and jumped to his feet, running through the room and out the door on the other side. He followed a long metal gantry over a cargo bay and went through the door on the other side.

Glancing around, Japheth quickly realised this was the end goal. There were no more doors in here. Just a large circular room filled with consoles wrapping around in consecutive circles.

The general was running between them, wildly hitting keypads and lighting up panels.

'That's enough, Xyan. It's over.'

The alien looked over to Japheth and shot his gun. Japheth ducked behind a terminal.

'It's not over until *I* say it is!'

Japheth slowly started moving alongside the console. 'Your ship is on emergency power. There's nothing you can do.'

A sickening laugh escaped the lips of the alien general. 'Actually, from the tactical defence consoles, I can release a barrage of nuclear missiles and blast the planet into shards.'

'You know I can't let you do that.' Japheth looked over the console but ducked back just in time to avoid the laser bolt that shot at him.

'I don't foresee a scenario in which you can stop me.'

He was right. Japheth couldn't get closer without getting shot. He needed a plan. With slow movements, Japheth worked his way behind a terminal and started yanking wires and components out of it. Dull tones started sounding as the general touched the keypad. 'What…what have you done!'

Japheth tucked himself in behind the machine as the general stalked round the room looking for him. As he walked past Japheth's hiding place, a hand reached out and hooked the general's foot, sending him hard to the ground. The gun bounced noiselessly along the carpeted floor.

In one swift movement, Japheth was out of his hiding place and on top of the general, raining fists in a flurry of blows aimed directly at his face.

Xyan attempted to protect his bloodied face with one arm while reaching with the other. Before Japheth could even reach, the general pointed a gun at his chest and fired.

Japheth felt the burning pain explode through him, fell backward, and hit the ground. His hands instinctively made their way to the open wound and pressed down as blood trickled through his fingers.

The general stood over him, looking down with a mix of pity and disdain. 'Humanity is weak. Pathetic. I will eradicate your kind from the universe if it's the last thing I do.'

Japheth looked up with wide eyes as the general spoke. 'But first, I'm going to find Alissa.' He slowly crouched beside the fallen man. 'I'm going to make her watch as I destroy the planet below, then I'm going to tear the other human apart in front of her eyes.' He was smiling now, enjoying the mental image of the torture he was about to inflict. 'And then…I'm going to kill her slowly. By the time I'm through with her, she will be begging me for death.'

Japheth felt his anger building inside him and reached for the general with a burst of adrenaline, pulling himself forward to smash his head against Xyan's face. Blood exploded from the alien's nose, and once more the gun was dropped.

A human hand wrapped around it, and with the last of his consciousness, Japheth fired the gun into the now bleeding face of the general. Xyan toppled lifelessly backwards, and Japheth's arm fell to the floor. 'Alissa…'

With a real effort, he reached up to his ear and connected his comms. 'Alissa…'

'Japheth?' Her voice sounded like music while he lay, fading into darkness. 'Alissa, I wanted to tell you…I love you.'

He could her the panic in her voice. 'Japheth? What's going on? Where are you?'

'I just wanted to hear your voice before…'

'Before what? Japheth? Answer me! Please!' He wanted to form words, but he felt the deep black creeping into his vision more and more. He lay there silently as he slipped into unconsciousness.

***

Alissa watched as the last of the general's guard fell. 'We need to find him, Shem!'

Shem nodded, and they ran, following Japheth's footsteps through the door and along the bridge into the large circular room.

Alissa brow furrowed as she surveyed the space around them. There was silence. 'Japheth?' Shem looked over at her then around the room. 'Oh, god, where is he?'

They both started running through the gaps between the consoles until Alissa finally spotted Japheth and the general, both blood-soaked, lying on the ground unmoving. A scream escaped her lips as she ran and dropped to her knees beside him. She pulled him up onto her knees and held him as Shem came running. 'Is he…dead?'

'I don't know.' The words came through tears as she looked down at Japheth's silent face then back up to Shem. 'Help him, please.'

Shem dropped down and took hold of Japheth's wrist. Alissa held her breath as she watched Shem intently. 'There's a pulse. He's still with us, for now.'

Alissa sniffled. 'What do we do?'

'I'm gonna get help, Al. You stay with him.' Shem rose to his feet and started running as Alissa held Japheth in her arms.

'Don't leave me, Japheth,' she sobbed. 'You're not supposed to die here. I love you...'

Within a few minutes, Shem came running back into the room, flanked by guards, and pointed to where Alissa sat. 'He's there, please...you have to save him.'

She looked up at Shem as the guards manoeuvred her away. He ran to her side and wrapped an arm around her shoulder. 'It's all right...he'll be all right.'

'Can you promise me that?'

Shem looked down at Japheth but didn't answer.

CHAPTER TWENTY-ONE

MEGAN LAY ON THE HOSPITAL BED ONCE MORE WITH her feet in stirrups. Ham stood by her head, holding her hand while two of the soldiers stood at the bottom of the bed, prepping her to give birth.

'Ma'am, we're only trained for field first aid, so you're gonna have to talk us through this.'

Megan nodded. 'Okay...we can do this...'

Her breathing was laboured, and Ham was trying to breath along with her like she had taught him. Reaching down, Megan felt for dilation. It was difficult, not being able to see, but this wasn't her first experience with childbirth. Although, it was very different from this side.

She cried out in pain and Ham gasped. 'What do I do?'

'Nothing, just keep breathing with me. All right, you two. It's time to start pushing.' Megan was speaking through gritted teeth. An animalistic growl came out of her mouth as she pushed.

'Ma'am, we can see the top of the head.'

Ham held tightly. 'Now push again?'

Megan nodded and pushed, crying out against the strain.

'Ma'am, the head is out.'

Megan paused, catching her breath. And through tears she began to push again. It was only a few more moments before the baby was out and being placed on Megan's chest.

'If I understand human anatomy then, that's a male.'

Megan laughed gently while looking down at the tiny life. 'He's my boy.'

Ham smiled. 'What's his name?'

Megan gently stroked the baby's face. 'His name is Clarke.'

'Like the captain's name?'

'Just like the captain's name.'

***

The blue-skinned medical staff surrounded Japheth and lifted him gently onto a floating stretcher, which followed them out of the room. Alissa jogged behind them as they rushed out, trying to stay as close as she could. Shem was by her side all the way to the medical unit.

As they passed through the ship, they saw wounded aliens being tended to and others being closed in large black bags. The fight was over, but the aftermath would stay with all of them for life.

It took only a few minutes for them to reach the large doors to the sick bay, and they all hurried inside. As Alissa tried to follow the doctors through another set of doors, one blocked her way. 'I'm sorry. You need to wait here.'

'No, I…'

Her voice trailed off as Shem put his hand on her shoulder. 'Let them do their jobs, Al.'

The doctor turned and followed the others out of sight. Alissa slumped into a chair and ran her hands over her face. Shem took the seat beside her and sighed deeply. 'You know, Al, I always thought, deep down that it would be you and me.'

She looked at her feet as he spoke, scared to make eye contact in case she started crying.

'It's just, when we met it made sense. You're beautiful, an amazing mechanic, and the best friend anyone could have asked for. In all the years we were friends, nothing ever came in between us.'

'Shem…' Alissa tried to interrupt.

'I gotta get this out, Al.'

She nodded and let him continue.

'I spent years being in love with you. The you that wore overalls and had grease stains on her forehead. The you that would trip over her own feet or sit sideways on a chair. But I never told you. And by the time I was brave enough, that version of you was gone and I didn't realise it. You're not the woman I fell in love with anymore, and that's not a bad thing, Al. I happen to think the person you've become is incredible. I think I'm starting to understand why things have been so hard for us. I miss my old friend, and I never gave this version of you a chance.

'So, I wanna be your friend. Like always. Because I think there is someone out there who loves you in a way I never could.'

He glanced over to the hospital doors, and Alissa followed his gaze, hoping to see someone come out.

After a moment of nothing, Alissa took hold of Shem's hand. 'Thank you.'

He nodded and smiled slightly as he squeezed her hand.

It took hours of pacing and stressing before the medical staff came back through to where Alissa and Shem sat. She leapt across the room to the doctor. 'Is he okay? Did you save him?'

'He's alive. But it's gonna take some time to heal.'

Alissa nodded along as Shem stepped beside her. 'Can she see him?'

'Yes, but not for too long. He needs his strength for the trip back to the city.'

Alissa followed the doctor through the doors and down a long corridor. Everything in there was so white. A stark contrast to the rest of the décor on the ship.

They arrived at a side room, and the doctor opened the door and allowed Alissa inside.

In the centre of the room, surrounded by wires and machines, lay Japheth. His eyes opened slightly as she walked closer, and he smiled. 'We did it.'

Alissa stood by his bed and took his hand in hers. 'Yeah, we did.'

Japheth surveyed the room. 'Where's Shem? Is he okay?'

'He's all right. He's waiting for us. The doctors are arranging transport for us all back to Drovia.'

Japheth relaxed back and sighed while Alissa gave his hand a squeeze. 'I thought I'd lost you.'

'I'm tougher than that.'

'I'm not.' Alissa blinked back tears. 'I'm in love with you, Japheth.'

'Really?'

Slowly, gently, Alissa leaned forward and placed a kiss on his lips. 'Really.'

***

The doors to the small ship slip opened and Alissa climbed in, followed by Shem and a doctor pushing Japheth in a metal chair. It had been three days since the end of the fight, and the medical staff had finally stabilised Japheth enough that he could travel back to the planet below.

It took just under an hour before the humans were back in the city. The ship docked in the hangar, and they were escorted straight to the hospital where Japheth was hooked up to innumerable machines. He looked at the wires surrounding him. 'Well, looks like I'm gonna be here a while. Why don't you guys go see Megan?'

'No need' came the voice from behind them.

As Alissa spun around, she saw her doctor friend in a wheelchair and carrying her baby. Ham stood behind, pushing her into the room.

'Oh my God! Megan!' Alissa rushed to her. 'I'm so glad you guys are okay.' She turned and wrapped Ham in her arms. He lifted her off the ground and squeezed her tightly, only putting her down so he could do the same with Shem.

Once Alissa was back on solid ground, she looked down at the baby. 'Megan...he's so beautiful.'

'Just like his daddy.' Alissa watched as tears slid down Megan's cheeks. 'Clarke would have loved him so much. Do you want to hold him?'

Alissa nodded gently, and Megan carefully handed her the baby. 'He's so tiny.'

The room watched as Alissa swayed from side to side and cooed at the little life in her arms. None more so than Japheth. He couldn't help the smile that spread across his face. After all that he'd been through, he never imagined a world in which he could have a life and a family. But now, anything seemed possible.

***

The emperor stood tall in front of the building that used to be City Hall with a sad look upon his face. Civilians gathered around in crowds to watch him speak for the first time since the battle.

'It is with deep sadness we stand here today, remembering the people we have lost. Both Drovian and humans came together against the Committee to protect our world, in an act of pure defiance against the cosmos itself.'

180

Alissa stood in the crowd with Japheth's hand wrapped around her own, watching the emperor speak, her eyes welling up when he mentioned the loss of life. She felt Garret's absence, and it was raw.

'Drovia is not now, and will never again be, targeted by the Unified Collective,' the emperor continued. 'Thanks to the actions of a few well-placed humans, a peace has been brokered. I would ask Alissa Namaah, Shem Mitchell, and Japheth Riordan to step up here please.'

Alissa looked at Japheth, who started making his way towards the stage, pulling her gently by the hand as he made his way through the crowd. As she turned back, Shem was following with a shy smile on his face.

As they moved, they could hear the crowd cheering for them, and by the time they reached the emperor, the collection of humans and drovians were cheering and clapping loudly.

'The three of you risked your lives to save us.' The emperor smiled as he spoke. 'Not only that, but you ensured this civilisation will forever be safe to thrive and grow.'

Alissa looked out over the grateful crowd and smiled. This was it. Humanity had found their New World.

THE END

ACKNOWLEDGEMENTS

This story could not have happened without the help of the following people.

Ken Dalrymple, for your constant support.
Paul Cringle, for the epic chapter images.
BNBS, for showing me how it's done.
Miblart, for the amazing cover art.
Sandra Ogle, for being a brilliant copy editor.

ABOUT THE AUTHOR

Jennifer Swift has been an avid science fiction fan for many years. Surrounding herself with books and TV shows that captured her imagination. From Star Trek to Red Dwarf, the idea of space travel has implanted itself deep within her mind, inspiring a series that not only stays true to science fiction, but offers an array of likeable and realistic characters that you can't help but become attached to